Seeking the Sun

Jason P. Crawford

DEDICATION

This book is dedicated to my wife, Cherrie Lynn. You are the light that shines in my life when all else is dark.

..

Praise for *Seeking the Sun*

"A captivating story of lost love, reclaimed passion, and tragic betrayal. I couldn't put it down until I finished the last word." – Jennifer R. McDonald, author of the *Veilwalker Trilogy*

ACKNOWLEDGMENTS

First, I wish to acknowledge Cassandre Bolan. Her gorgeous cover graces the front of this book and is exactly what I wanted to see. Thank you!

I would also like to thank my beta readers—Cherrie Lynn, Ann Elena Fors, Ren Buidhe, Jennifer R. McDonald, and Tarsha Brown. You helped me make my story so much better.

Finally, I want to thank you, my readers. I hope you enjoy.

Prologue

The woman ran, and the man pursued her.

Through the forest, her feet pounded, snagging on tendrils and roots and smashing into clover as her heart crashed against her chest in the same rhythm. Her lungs ached, heart burning as though it had been shot through.

No. Her thoughts were wild, those of the hunted animal. *He can't catch me. Not him. Anyone but him.*

She could hear his breathing, getting closer and closer as he chased her. His green eyes caught glimpses of her fleeing form, and the sight drove him like the master's whip, frenzied and wild. He clawed at the trees and branches which obstructed him, and they gave way with loud *snaps*.

"Father!" Her voice was shrill and panicked. She could smell the man's breath and sweat, he was so close; victory shone in his face as he reached for her. "Father! Save me!"

Chapter One

"Come on, slowpoke! We're not going to make it!"

Daphne groaned and rubbed her eyes as she rolled out of her bed. She struggled against the quilts which had wrapped around her during the night; in Maine, it got chilly at night even during the summer.

"Can't we wait until tomorrow?" Her eyelids felt like they had lead weights pulling them down. "It's not like they're gonna rent my dorm out or something, you know."

"Wanna bet?" Her mother, Carolyn, pushed open the door to Daphne's bedroom and flipped on the light. The flood of illumination caused the young woman to throw her arm over her eyes and moan.

Carolyn grinned as she started pulling the black-out curtains off the rod and folding them up.

"I remember when I went to university." She shook her head, smiling at the memories. "I was twenty minutes late for dorm room assignments because my dad insisted on checking the oil for the fifth time. Almost didn't get a spot."

"Oh, no." Daphne's voice was muted by her arm and the sheets. "Not the 'pushed-the-cheerleader-out-of-the-way' story again. I don't think I can take it."

Carolyn tucked the curtain under her arm. "Then maybe you'd better get out of bed, young lady." She paused on the way out the door. "Every five minutes we're waiting for you is five minutes more you'll have to listen to me talk about my old school days." She smiled. "...or your father about the time he listened to that Carl Sagan lecture about astrophysics."

"Gaak!" Daphne jumped out of bed.

The sun sparkled on her long red hair as she ran to her wall mirror. She grabbed for her hairbrush, but her fingers closed around empty air.

"Hey! Where did it go?"

"In the box. That's what happens when you sleep too late—all of your stuff ends up in boxes while you snore the morning away."

"Mom!" Daphne turned back to the mirror and started combing her fingers through her hair in a desperate attempt to tame the waves. Her blue eyes were bloodshot and her pale skin was marked by the imprint of her wool pajamas where she had lain on her arm.

"Nope. Sorry. Buried underneath your DVDs." Carolyn had begun walking down the stairs. "Breakf...lunch is ready when you come down."

"Are you serious?" Daphne turned to rush after her mother. "You expect me..."

A flash of reflected light caught her attention. Blinking, she turned in its direction.

On her bedside table rested a box. A silver handle peeked out from the open top.

She couldn't hold back the smile. *Got me.* Withdrawing the brush, she began passing it through the bright copper which adorned her head, working her way through knots and snarls until what had been a frizzled nightmare had become almost liquid, flowing its way to the middle of her back. Another few moments and her purple wool was replaced with a knee-length pleated skirt and cream-colored blouse. She squinted at the mirror and shook her head.

And, at last, the finishing touch. Returning to her bedside, Daphne opened the drawer and removed a pair of wire-frames. She held them to the light, looking for smudges or dirt, then slid them over her ears and up her nose. One more glance in the mirror, and she was out the door and heading downstairs.

~~~

"She lives!"

"Ha, ha, Mom." Daphne placed her seedling tree on a counter, grabbed a plate from the cupboard, and started scooping eggs from a casserole dish. "Is there any bacon or corned beef?"

"Might be able to dig some up." Her father walked in from the adjacent living room. His voice trembled as he spoke. "Probably need to heat it up, though."

Daphne and her mother shared a meaningful glance; the older woman smiled and traced a line down from the corner of her eye. Her daughter nod-ded.

"Thanks, Dad." The mood leading up to the cli-chéd "car-trip-to-college" had been one of anxious excitement, filled with activity and preparations on all sides. Daphne had checked and double-checked her acceptance letter and the welcome packet she had received in the mail to ensure that they knew exactly where they were going; both were headed by a smiling Florida gator that made her smile when she saw it. Her father, Charles, had spent his spare time making sure that their route was clear and planning out their rest stops.
~~~

Daphne sat down and rubbed her eyes. "Man, I'm tired. Sometimes I wish that the sun didn't rise till noon." She stretched and yawned.

"What were you up to last night?" Carolyn broke in on Daphne's thoughts. "You were up awfully late."

"Just couldn't sleep. Excited." A shrug. "Working on some of my story ideas, trying to put together an outline." She acted like she didn't hear her mother's sigh. "When I finally conked out, it was like I woke up as soon as my eyes closed. Plus I knew we didn't have to leave until this afternoon anyway, since we're stopping at a hotel on the way there."

"Well..."

Charles' voice interrupted Carolyn. "Better early than late, princess."

"You're not a king, dad, so I'm not a princess!"

"No, but your mother's a queen. So there." Her father, the man who had given her both her red hair and her nearsightedness, peeked over his paper. His face was mostly hidden behind the news, but his eyes twinkled over the corner he had folded in.

"Real mature, Dad." Daphne rolled her eyes. "'So there?' What's next? Sticking out your tongue?" To demonstrate, she did just that, waggling it from side to side.

No answer came for a moment, then they all laughed. The laugh went on longer than one would expect, and tears welled up in more than one pair of eyes. Charles tossed his paper onto the table and swept his daughter up in a big hug.

"I'm going to miss you, baby girl."

"I'll miss you too, Dad." Daphne leaned back and smiled into her dad's quivering face. "But I'll come home for the holidays and stuff, you know. Don't worry too much."

"We can't help worrying, sweetie." Carolyn dabbed at her own eyes. "We're parents. It's what we do, especially when our little girl is headed out into the great big world all by herself."

"Plus, who's going to take care of that baby tree while you study your head off?" Charles shook his head as he leaned out from his chair and over the pot which held Daphne's laurel sapling. "What have you been feeding this thing, princess? It's growing like crazy!"

Daphne shook her head and chuckled. "Guys, knock it off. Dad, the tree is fine, I'm just keeping it watered and adding plant food. Both of you—it's just *school*. It's not like I'll be trying to work or live off campus or anything. I'm just going to be in a dorm room, probably with a roommate who I can't stand and who can't stand me, and I'll be wishing I could come back home in two weeks." She pulled free from her father's embrace and shrugged. "It'll be just like an extended summer camp or something."

Both parents stared at her; her father was the first to break the silence. "Hey, speaking of summer camps, it looks like it'll be a hotter one next year." He picked up the paper and flipped a few pages, then pointed to a headline in one of the columns.

Daphne and her mother leaned in to peer at the text. It read SOLAR ACTIVITY REACHES HIGHEST POINT IN 50 YEARS. ASTRONOMERS BAFFLED.

"Dad, I don't *think* that that means that the temperature is going to be higher next year." She took the paper and scanned it. "Nope. Just talking about solar flares and sunspots. Looks like they picked up way ahead of schedule, and lots more than were expected. Weird."

"Look," Carolyn picked up her husband's plate and walked it to the sink, "we've still got some packing to do if we're going to make it to that hotel in time for everyone to get a good night's sleep before tomorrow morning. Eat your breakfast!"

"Lunch, you mean." Daphne winked, then laughed before stuffing her mouth full of eggs.

Chapter Two

I can't move.

I can't feel.

Why?

A strange caress on her skin, her face, traces over rough edges with such care and love.

"You will never grow old." It is *his* voice, and, even now, she cringes back from it, recoils without moving. She can no longer see him, no longer smell him, but she knows that it is him.

Her pursuer.

"You will be my symbol, sacred, forever." His hands reach up, rubbing along the smoother skin of her arms and fingers before he bends one back upon itself.

She tries to scream, but cannot. She has no mouth.

Her arm snaps.

~~~

Daphne's eyes flew open as her cheek bumped into something cold and hard; her hands clutched around the solid shape of her tree pot in her lap.

"Wakey wakey." Her father's eyes sparkled in the rear-view mirror. "Might want to wipe that drool off your chin before all the college guys get their first look at you, princess."

"You're not a king, Dad, so I'm not a princess." Her voice sounded like it was coming through a pillow as she pulled her hand across her lower lip. Part of her mind was still trapped in that strange dream, and she flexed her fingers to make sure that they were still there. Her eyes turned toward the window, and the last vestiges of fog were banished as she took in the sights before her.

Thousands of people were swarming over the college campus; green fields were covered in banners trumpeting the worth of this or that organization, and sidewalks teemed with parents
~~~

and siblings munching on hot dogs and burgers while students filled out interest forms or looked at pamphlets and fliers. The school mascot stood in the shade as much as possible. Daphne winced at the thought of how much he must be sweating in that giant alligator suit. The sounds of the crowd merged into one flow, almost fluid as it cascaded over her ears.

"Not bad." Charles nodded his head as he stepped off the path to avoid bumping into a young man whose head was buried in his campus map. "So this is the University of Florida."

"That's right." Carolyn's grin threatened to over-take her face. "Our baby got a full scholarship to one of the best schools in the world." She leaned over and gave Daphne a giant hug; the girl resisted the urge to squirm away. "You know we're so proud of you, right, hon?"

Daphne rolled her eyes, but her smile was full of affection. "I know, Mom. I know." She reached into her skirt pocket and came back with her own map. "I guess we need to head that way." She pointed to-ward one of the nearby buildings. "They'll set me up with my schedule and let me know which dorm building I'm supposed to be in."

"Didn't you already register for that online?"

Daphne nodded. "Still better to make sure. I'd hate to head all the way over to the Weaver Building and find out I'm not supposed to be there after all."

"Well." Charles squared his shoulders and picked up two of Daphne's bags again. "Let's get a move on, then; I'm sure you'll need time to settle in and all."

Daphne put her arm around her father and gave him a quick peck on the cheek; his eyes blinked several times before he smiled.

"I love you, Dad. Relax, we've got plenty of time; I was hoping you guys would at least be here for dinner."

Charles looked down as he spoke. "Well, I guess. I mean..."

"That'd be great." Carolyn kissed her husband's other cheek. "Your father is just being emotionally handicapped again."

"I'm standing right here!"

"It wouldn't be any fun if you weren't." A round of laughter swept through the little group; a couple of passers-by smiled as they looked on.

"All right, all right." Charles adjusted the loads in his hands. "Let's move."

~~~

"Weaver Hall...Weaver Hall...Ah! There it is!" Daphne scanned her map, then pointed when she had found their destination. "Awesome! Looks like it's in a great spot on campus, too."
~~~

"Why there, hon?" Carolyn glanced behind them; Charles had begun huffing as he tried to keep up. "Do you need help, Charles?"

He shook his head, but his face had gone red and sweat was staining his collar. "No...I...I'm fine...Exercise is good for me, right?"

"Maybe you'll reconsider that gym membership when you get home, Dad!" A smirk. "Anyway, I wanted Weaver because that's where the International Exchange Program students are housed. If I'm lucky, I'll get to meet all sorts of people from different countries and stuff. It'll be great for my writing!" She stuck her nose up in the air. "After all, that's why I took all those foreign language courses from Rosetta Stone."

Carolyn sighed. "Honey, I know we've talked about this, but it's almost impossible to earn a living as a writer, especially nowadays with all those e-books and stuff. Don't you think..."

Daphne frowned, and Carolyn stopped. "I'm sorry, hon. You're right. This is your day, and it's your life. Your Dad and I just want..."

"You want what's best for me, I know." Daphne's blue eyes, a sharp contrast to her red-gold waves, flashed in her mother's direction. "But this is what got me into this school, Mom. They liked my essay, and their English department said that I have real potential as a writer. It's what I love doing, putting stories down on paper, and I am going to find a way to make it work."

"I know, I know." Another sigh. "It's just...we worry."

Daphne's harsh gaze softened. "I know you do. But don't." She tilted her head and smiled. "Or, at least, don't worry too much. I mean, I've got plenty of time to decide otherwise, right?"

Carolyn answered her daughter's smile. "But you won't. You're my daughter, after all."

"Fair enough."

The trio stopped in front of a four-story brick building. Bicycles were chained up in a rack in front of the structure, and there was a large white awning that stretched partway over the sidewalk leading up to the entrance. A welcoming table had been set up near the doorway. A pair each of men and women wearing UF Gator shirts and large smiles were checking rosters and directing incoming students to their rooms.

"Hi!" A young woman of Asian descent holding a clipboard approached the trio. "Are you registered for Weaver Hall?" Daphne nodded. "I'm Sayaka, and I'll be your RA this year. Do you know which room you've been assigned?"

"Not yet." Daphne brushed back a strand of her coppery hair.

"Name?"

"Daphne Gianakos."

A puzzled glance. "How do you spell that?"

Daphne sighed. "G...I...A...N...A...K...O...S."

"Oh! Here you are!" The greeter slid her finger across her roster to link Daphne's name with her room assignment. "Okay, you'll be on the second floor, Room 207. It's a double room, so you'll be with..." The girl squinted at the paper, then shook her head. "I don't know how to pronounce this name either. Anyway, she's already there, so you can ask her when you arrive." She handed Daphne a key marked 207.

As Daphne nodded and began to turn away, Sayaka held out a document. "This is the copy of our community rules. It has everything you need to know about visitations, complaint procedures, whatever. You'll find a nametag sticker inside to help you 'break the ice' with the other residents. If you have any questions, let me know! Welcome to the University of Florida!"

"Thank you." Daphne smiled and waved as Sayaka walked away; when she turned around, she shrugged before speaking. "Anyway, I guess I should probably head up there by myself if my roomie's already here. Don't want to freak her out with the parental units when we first meet." She flipped through the magazine and found the sticker; it was bright blue, and ensured that everyone who saw it knew the wearer was happy to see them.

Daphne sighed as she stuck it to her chest. "Just feels wrong for someone to give me a nametag and not to wear it...like I'm throwing away food or something."

"You think bringing us would 'freak her out'?" The smile on Charles' face gave the lie to his indignant words. "We're only the people who raised you from when you tried to eat crayons and Play-Doh, after all!"

"Dad. Knock it off." Daphne's face lit up as she remembered something. "Oh, right! I'm going to leave my tree in the car until this evening, okay? I don't want to make two trips just now and keep you guys stuck here."

"Okay, okay." Charles handed over the baggage, shaking his head as his daughter shouldered the weight with more ease than he had. "I guess it's all right. We'll have a look around and meet you at that chicken place we saw, okay? Say...an hour?"

Daphne nodded. "Make it two. I want to settle in a bit, get some things unpacked, make sure my roommate isn't planning to off me in my sleep, that sort of thing."

"Hon, you do have an imagination, don't you?" Carolyn gave her daughter another hug. "See you in a couple of hours. Have fun!"

"Sure will!" Daphne waved as her parents turned and walked away, but when they had gone, the smile dropped off her face and the nervousness which she had been feeling in her stomach all day finally displaced her determined cheerfulness. She tried to walk in the door, but it suddenly seemed so far away. There was an ache, a burning, in her chest as she looked at the dorm.

I'm afraid. She put her bags down and wiped her sweaty palms on her shirt. *Why am I afraid? It's just college.* She closed her eyes. *Come on, Daphne. Get moving. They're just people. Just like in a story. Just people.*

She opened her eyes and tried again to get her feet moving. This time it worked, and, as step followed step, the door no longer seemed quite so ominous and forbidding, although the burn in her heart remained. She walked into the building with her head held high and her blue eyes glinting.

Chapter Three

The lobby of the International Hall was filled with a scene resembling a Middle-Eastern swap meet. Older, out-going students were offering their wares to incoming freshmen—a set of silverware here, a CD-player there—and the commotion was enough to make Daphne wince as she came through the door. A sign over the setup proclaimed "Weaver International Recycling Program—First Come, First Served."

"They're not for you." Turning, Daphne saw another student with raven-black hair and a white blouse. The girl wore a pair of designer sunglasses, and they contrasted with her pale skin.

"Excuse me?"

"These are for the exchange students." The young woman turned her face toward Daphne, and removed her sunglasses.

Her eyes were completely white.

Daphne gasped and held a hand over her mouth; the corner of the other girl's mouth twisted upward at the sound.

"I'm always glad when I hear that sound, as it tells me, at least, that I am in the company of someone who is as shocked by what has befallen me as I am." She extended her hand. "My name is Cassandra."

A moment's pause, then Daphne reached out to take it in her own. "I'm..."

"Daphne Gianakos. I know."

Daphne snatched her hand out of Cassandra's grasp. "How did you..."

Cassandra pointed at Daphne's chest. The younger girl followed Cassandra's finger.

It was leveled at the nametag she wore.

"You...but...I thought..."

"You thought I was blind." Cassandra sighed. "Of course you did; everyone does. Sometimes I milk it for a while, watching them while they don't know it, but I thought it would be more fun to give you the 'mind-reader' shock." She flashed a wicked smile. "It was."

Daphne's heart was beginning to return to a more normal rhythm, but it was taking some effort for her to not fly off and either start yelling or storm off. "That...that wasn't funny, Cassandra."

Cassandra's smile did not fade. "I thought it was." She flicked her hair away from her eyes. "Anyway, like I was saying, the recycle program is for the exchange students; they usually can't bring everything over from the country they came from, so the people on the way out hold this giveaway every year so that they can pick up some of the things that they need but had to leave behind."

"Oh." Daphne looked around again at the crowd. "That's nice. I like that idea."

"Of course. You should be careful, though." Cassandra turned her white-eyed gaze once more onto Daphne, and this time, the lines around her eyes had faded, and her gaze was soft. "You are holding an arrow in your chest, your hands around the shaft. You scream as you remove it from your breast, and your life pours out onto the dirt."

Daphne took a step back. "What the hell..."

Cassandra's eyes scrunched closed, then reopened. She examined Daphne with...curiosity? Respect?

Daphne stared for a moment, then laughed. "Whatever." She crossed her arms in front of her chest. "You're crazy...or just messing with me. What is this, some kind of sorority initiation?" She turned away and began jogging for the staircase, glancing back once to see the older girl still standing in the lobby, staring after her.

Cassandra's lips moved, but Daphne could not hear what she said.

~~~

Daphne stumbled through the hallways, trying to calm herself, trying not to run...but something made it difficult.

She was just screwing with me. Why am I so frightened?

She passed her room twice, turning around each time when she realized her mistake, before she found it—207. The sound of rock music filtered through the wooden paneling. The door was shut, so Daphne pulled out her key and turned it in the lock.

Click.

She began to turn the doorknob, but before she could even finish the turn, the door was pulled open from the other side and she was swept into a bear hug by someone who smelled like lavender.

"Ohmigod!" The mystery hugger bounced up and down while embracing Daphne. "Are you my roommate? It's going to be so awesome! I'm soooo
~~~

glad you're here; we're going to need to talk about all sorts of things, like decorations, and boys..."

Daphne was on the verge of passing out from lack of oxygen before the other girl let go. Taking a deep breath as she sank to sit in the nearest chair, she tried a smile, but it felt weak on her face. Her roommate did not notice, however; she simply kept talking as she moved about the room in her pale yellow pajama shorts and top.

"I hope you don't mind, but I took this bed, over by this window." The girl pointed to the room's portal to the outdoors, overlooking the lawn toward the library. "It's cause that's got the better view of the outside. I get nervous if I can't see the outside. It's not like I have claustrophobia, or whatever, it's just that the inside feels all sticky and it's hard to breathe. Hey, do you like Pepsi? I hope so, cause that's my favorite kind of soda and I don't want all of our fridge space to be taken up by two different ones. I feel more comfortable in pajamas, so I'll probably be in those most of the time I'm in the room. If you want, I can..."

Daphne stood up and held her hands out in the age-old "stop" gesture. "Hey. Before we start talking about soda-sharing arrangements, shouldn't we at least introduce ourselves?" She held out her hand. "I'm Daphne. I'm an English major."

The speed-talking towhead gaped at Daphne for a moment, then covered her mouth and giggled.

"I'm sorry." She took Daphne's hand and shook it. "I'm just so nervous. My name is Clytia, but call me Chloe. It's much easier for everyone. I'm working on a degree in psych."

Daphne cocked her head. "That's a name I've never heard before. Does it mean something? Where does it come from?"

Chloe rolled her eyes. "My parents are big literature and mythology freaks. They named my brother Hector, my sister Pandora."

Daphne blinked. "Really? Don't all those characters die in terrible ways?"

"Well, the stories don't really say what happened to Pandora." Chloe sat down on her bed. "But, yeah, they like the 'tragic characters.' They said that they hope it drives us to do better." In response to Daphne's confused look, she laughed. "Yeah. Exactly what we said."

"So what's the story behind your name?"

"Oh, that. Okay." The girl took a deep breath and began speaking in the tones of someone reciting a verse they have been forced to memorize. "Clytia loved the sun, but he loved her sister Leucothea. When Clytia realized that he had been masquerading as Leucothea's husband in order to get into her sister's bedroom, she told their father. Her father had Leucothea buried alive, but the sun did not fall in love with Clytia. He continued to reject her, and, when she died, he turned her into the *heliotrope*."

"The what?"

"It's some sort of sunflower-type thing. Basically, she was cursed to always follow the sun, like she had in her life, but it would always ignore her, carrying on its merry way."

"Wow."

"Yeah."

A moment of silence passed between the two girls before Daphne spoke again. "At least they didn't name your sister Leucothea."

Chloe gaped at her, then began laughing. Daphne joined in, and the room was filled with squeals.

"Yeah." Chloe forced the words out between laughs. "I guess they figured they'd given us enough bad juju."

Another chuckle. "Hey, my parents are hanging around for dinner tonight." Daphne sat back up. "Do you want to come? I'm sure they'd love talking crazy literature and whatnot with you."

Chloe winced. "Thanks, but no; I've already got plans to go into town and start binge-shopping for stuff for the room. But see you when I get back?"

Daphne smiled. "Yeah. Pick up a good movie while you're at it. We can watch it in the lounge."

"Sounds great."

Chapter Four

"Sounds like you've got a good roommate set-up." Charles gestured with his half-eaten drumstick. "When I was in college, I had a roommate with some sort of uncontrollable growth between his toes."

"Charles! We're eating!" Carolyn's lips puckered up in a *moue* of disgust. "Do you need to talk about that at the table?"

"Well...no, I suppose not." The smile disappeared and Charles' face became downcast.

Three seconds passed.

"But I *can*." His pout turned into a wicked grin and he winked at his wife and daughter. "It's one of the privileges of growing older."

"Well, Dad, you can go ahead and try, but you can't gross me out or mess with my day." Daphne scooped another spoonful of macaroni and cheese into her mouth.

"Don't tempt me, princess."

"You're not a king, Dad." The customary response came mumbled around a mouthful of pasta. A swallow, then, "I am having the best day ever. I'm finally at my school, I've got a great roommate and I think we're going to really get along...and I've even gotten a few ideas for a book!" She shook her head, still smiling. "I thought that today was going to be scary, but, for the most part, it's been awesome."

"Honey, that's great!" Carolyn reached over and gave her daughter a hug. "I hope that you still feel that way after you've been here a few weeks."

"Well, I know it's not going to be sunshine and roses all the time. Studying, roommate stress, whatever. Still." She finished her macaroni and turned to her chicken. "It's a good start."

"What about that weird girl?" Her father wiped his mouth as he set down his Diet Coke. "The one in the dorm?"

"They're called 'Residence Halls,' Dad." Daphne shuddered, remembering the blank look in Cassandra's eyes. "Yeah, that *was* weird." She rubbed her left arm as if she were chilled. "I don't know what that was all about, but she was probably just pranking me, trying to freak out a new girl."

"Maybe it *was* a sorority initiation." Carolyn put her fork back into her chicken jambalaya when Daphne paused to sip her water. "I remember, when I was in school, some of those got really...strange. Things that no one in their right minds would do as an adult."

Charles nodded. "Same with fraternities—making the pledges do crazy things just for the privilege of being considered for membership." He shook his head. "Not something I ever understood myself."

"It's the urge to belong to something larger than yourself, dear." Carolyn put her hand on her husband's. "Some people are just afraid of the new college environment and are looking for something to latch on to, to help them feel secure."

"Sure, and they subject themselves to torments and torture in order to 'fit in.'" Charles punctuated his comment with air-quotes. "It's disgusting, this need that kids seem to have to fit in with the mob."

"Dad, I'd really rather not turn this into a discussion on how bad kids are and how much better it was back when you were young." Daphne shook her head. "The world is a different place now."

"You make me feel old when you say that, princess."

"Didn't you just comment on the privileges of getting older, Dad?"

The moment stretched out, until everyone at the table burst into laughter.

~~~

"Well, we need to get going." Carolyn sighed as Charles slid his Visa into the billfold. "We've got a long drive ahead and we want to get as far as we can before we need to sleep."

"Okay." Daphne stood and walked around to her parents, giving them each a hug and a kiss on the cheek. "I love you guys. I'm going to miss you, but I think that this is going to work out. I'm going to be all right."

"We know you are." Charles clapped his daughter on the shoulder, and Carolyn nodded and wiped away glistening tears. "We're very proud of you, Daphne. You've grown into a fine young woman."

Daphne found her throat closing up. "Thanks, Dad. Mom." The trio walked toward the door, the silence a mark of their moods. "I guess...I guess I'll see you guys later."

"We're not leaving just yet." Charles folded his arm and glowered at his daughter. "We need to drop you off and you need to get that tree out of my backseat!"
~~~

~~~

It was after ten o'clock when Daphne got back to Weaver Hall. She paused at door 207 and pressed her ear against the wood. She heard nothing.

Either she's not home or she's already asleep, I guess.

She put her seedling down and brought out her key, but a sudden whispering caught her ear, and she leaned in to the door again.

The person inside was speaking in Greek.

"No, I haven't seen him yet." The voice on the other side was low, soft. "But you're sure? No mistakes this time?"

Several moments passed.

"No, I know what to look for. What? All right. Goodbye."

Daphne's brow furrowed. Sounds of someone moving around were followed by a sudden blast of music.

She inserted her key and opened up the door, peeking her head around to see who was in the room.

"Hi!" Chloe bounded toward the door when she saw Daphne. "How was dinner with your family? Did they get all teary-eyed and stuff? I know I did when mine left." She leaned around Daphne. "Hey, is that a tree? Awesome! Are we allowed to keep trees in here? Did you want to see the movie I got?"
~~~

A moment passed as Daphne stared at Chloe digging around in her Target bag for the DVD she had bought. The blonde girl held up a copy of *Thor* and turned back.

"I thought that a good, hot superhero might be just the thing." Chloe stared at the front of the box and trailed her fingers across Chris Hemsworth's face, sighing. Then she blinked, and the smile dropped off her face. "Is something wrong, Daphne?"

"No, it was just..." She shook her head, then came back with a small smile. "Everything's fine. I guess I was just a little preoccupied with my parents leaving and stuff."

Chloe's sunny face returned. "Sure! Of course you are! Hey, why don't we go watch Chris be all muscly and stuff while he swings a giant hammer? I bet that'll cheer you up!"

"You're on!" The pair left and locked the room. "How did you know I was a big superhero buff?"

Chloe shrugged as they walked down the hallway toward the lounge. "I didn't."

Then she gave Daphne a wicked smile. "But I figured that I couldn't go wrong with sexy guys, so..."

Daphne slapped her friend on the shoulder as they dissolved into more laughter. "Is that all you think about?"

Chloe drew herself up and spread her fingers out over her chest. "Of course not! It's only *most* of what I think about!"

The two roommates settled in next to each other on the small couch in front of the big-screen TV. There were a few other girls walking to and fro from one room to another.

As the titles began to roll, Daphne nudged her friend. "Hey." She extended a finger. "What's her problem?"

She was pointing at Cassandra, who stood in an open doorway, her eyes fixed on the pair. As Chloe turned, Cassandra disappeared, and Daphne could hear the door *click* behind her.

"I don't know." Chloe's brows were pinched and furrowed. Her voice was low and measured, as if explaining something to a child. "She's strange. She says really weird things to people...terrible things, you know? Like about how they're going to break up, or have accidents, or whatever."

Daphne shuddered as the encounter from earlier that day echoed in her mind. "She jumped me this afternoon, when I first got over here." Visions of the girl's white eyes flashed across Daphne's imagination. "She told me that...what was it? I would have to pull an arrow out of my chest, or something." She rubbed her hands on her arms as the chill in her spirit reached her flesh. "Isn't that crazy?"

When Chloe did not respond, Daphne glanced up at her face...and the chills worsened. Chloe was very pale, and her eyes darted back and forth as they looked at nothing, and her lips moved in silent speech.

"Chloe?" No immediate answer. "Chloe? Chloe!" Daphne put her hand on her roommate's shoulder and shook her. "Wake up! What's wrong?"

Chloe seemed to come out of a reverie. "I...she just has a bad reputation. The stuff that she says usually comes true, you know? It's creepy and weird."

Daphne couldn't tell whether her new friend was just teasing her or not, but, looking into Chloe's face, she didn't think it was a prank. "Are you saying..."

"What?" Chloe shook her head. "No! I don't think she's ever said that someone was actually going to *die* before and had it come true. I mean, if she had, she'd be questioned by the police and stuff for how she knew, right?"

"I...I don't know..."

"Anyway, there's no way that you're gonna keel over or something. I mean, even if she *is* right, you'd have to meet someone who wanted to shoot you in the chest with an arrow. Or someone who's critically clumsy. Is there anyone who fits the bill?" Chloe's mouth twitched in a smirk.

Daphne shook her head. "I don't even like *watching* archery."

Chloe nodded and leaned back in her seat. "All right then, no sweat." She nodded again. "I mean, not like it was *going* to happen if you did, you understand, but now it's definitely *definitely* not going to happen, you know?"

Daphne laughed, but it was more a nervous titter than a genuine chuckle. "Sure. Nothing like getting a death prophecy on your first day away from home, you know?"

"Hey, don't worry! I've got the cure for the creepie-girlies!" She reached into the couch cushions and produced a remote control. "Hot superheroes!"

Chapter Five

"So how're your classes going?" Chloe asked as Daphne closed the door. "Seems like you've been working hard all week."

"Yeesh." Daphne sank into her chair. "I knew that I wasn't really prepared for college by high school, you know, but I had no idea just *how* unprepared I would be."

"You'll get used to it." Chloe tied her hair into a short ponytail.

"You sure seem to have." Daphne shook her head as she pulled out book after book from her messenger bag. "I never see you doing any homework or anything."

Chloe shrugged. "What can I say? I'm a super genius."

The two ladies laughed for a few moments. When the joviality subsided, Chloe strolled over to the refrigerator and pulled out a Pepsi. The *hiss* of carbonation filled the room.

"Any more meetings with Miss Creepy?"

"Cassandra?" Daphne shook her head. "Nope, haven't seen her at all, which is fine by me."

"No kidding." The blonde took a swig of her soda, and sighed. "Hey, look."

Daphne turned her head; Chloe was indicating the seedling tree she had brought from home. It had grown an inch over the last week.

"I know." Daphne reached out to touch one of its smooth, knife-shaped leaves. "It's growing like crazy over here. Maybe there's something in the air or the water."

"Nah. It's the sunshine." Chloe threw open the drapes to let in more of the daylight. "See? Isn't this better than Maine?"

"It's warmer, that's for sure." Daphne opened up her English folder, running her finger through the syllabus. "I'm not sure that I like so much direct sunlight, though. I keep worrying that I'll burn."

Chloe laughed as she spoke. "Well, you are pretty light. Don't want to come out looking like a lobster or anything."

Daphne shook her head again, color rising in her cheek. "Yeah. It's a bit surprising; my grandfather was Greek and they have that nice Mediterranean skin, but I guess it skipped a generation or something."

"Greek, huh? Is that where you get that crazy last name?"

"Yep." Daphne reached into the bag again and pulled out her new Kindle. A few clicks later, she was paging through Oscar Wilde's *The Painting of Dorian Gray*.

"Like the tablet better than a paper book?"

Daphne nodded as she skimmed through the first few pages. "My parents prefer paper, of course, but I like being able to carry dozens of books in one tablet. Makes reading and research a heck of a lot easier, you know?"

"Sure. Hey, I heard that someone is holding a big 'welcome to college' party tonight. Supposed to be tons of people, loud music..." She nudged Daphne with her elbow, almost making her drop her Kindle. "...boys."

Daphne rolled her eyes. "Chloe, while I appreciate the intention, I'm here to get an actual education and learn how to be a better writer, not to hook up with every male creature on campus."

"Great! More for me!" The sincerity in Chloe's voice made Daphne jerk her head up to look at her friend; when their eyes met, a huge smile stretched across Chloe's face as she dropped Daphne an exaggerated wink. The two chuckled.

"Seriously, though, Daphne." Chloe sat down next to her roommate, took the tablet out of her hands, and then took those hands in her own. "If you don't go, who's going to make sure I don't get myself in too much trouble?" She did her best to make Puss-in-Boots eyes at Daphne. "I'll be like a little, pathetic, vulnerable kitten, all by myself with no one to take care of me. Anyone who wants to could just carry me off and take advantage of my sweet innocence."

"See, there you go." Daphne *tsked*. "You had a good argument right up until you claimed some sort of innocence."

"How dare you!" Chloe stuck her nose in the air. "There are several things that I *haven't* tried, thank you very much!"

"Oh, yeah? Name three."

Chloe tapped the side of her nose with her finger. "Nope."

Another laugh. "Fine! Fine!" Daphne threw her hands up in the air in mock annoyance. "I'll come, if it'll make you happy. You're right. You would just be a target for anyone trying to get a piece of ass, anyway."

"So vulgar! I'm proud of you!"

"Yeah, yeah." Daphne snatched her tablet back. "When is this party, anyway?"

"Starts at 8. Goes until whenever. It *is* Friday, after all."

Daphne smiled, taking out a notepad and pen. "Fridays are good days." She looked back at her roommate. "I'll be there. I promise. Don't you worry about me."

"I'll hold you to it," Chloe replied. "Just follow all the music and bright lights."

~~~

Daphne turned off her tablet and stretched. *So easy to get lost while reading*, she thought. *Hope I'm not...*

She glanced at the time on her phone.

7:47.

"Ah, shit!" She snatched up her tablet, tossed on her shoes, and glanced at herself in the mirror. "Gonna have to be good enough, cause Chloe'll kill me if I'm not there!"

Daphne dashed through the hallway, sprinting for the stairs. As she ran, she felt a chill run down her back.

She glanced behind her.
~~~

Cassandra was staring after her, staring from a doorway again, her blank eyes following Daphne as she moved.

"What is your *problem?!*" Daphne yelled as she passed.

"Better hurry." The reply drifted on the wind like smoke. "You're going to be late."

~~~

Daphne ran through the night, squinting her eyes against the constant adjustment between light and dark. The campus had a large amount of lamps and the buildings were easy to find, but any time she glanced down or away her eyes watered and she winced.

"Damn it." Her hair flowed in the wind and she tried to shield her eyes from the glare as she looked round to get her bearings. "Which one..."

Her thought was interrupted as she caught a glimpse of someone standing in the glow of a street-light. From this distance, he was hard to see, but something about him captured Daphne's attention...resulting in her setting a foot down on a round rock and stumbling off her feet and onto her back. Her glasses landed in the grass beside her. The breath was forced from her body, and she lay unable to move.
~~~

As Daphne lay on the ground trying to catch her breath, she heard footsteps approaching. "Are you alright?" The figure she had seen leaned over her, looking down into her face. He was a young man, his strong features framed by curly blonde hair that reached to his shoulders. He was dressed for the Florida summer, in shorts and T-shirt, and his face was filled with a concerned smile that revealed flawless teeth.

"Wh..." Daphne's hand closed around her glasses as she tried to speak, but the spasms of her chest prevented her from completing a word. At the sound, however, the strange man narrowed his eyes.

Daphne's glasses found her face.

Time stopped.

It's him. She stared into his green eyes, and fear flooded her brain. *The one from my dream.*

The concern and kindness in his face melted away, to be replaced by a look of disbelief. His brow unknotted, his face smoothed, and his eyes crinkled as he knelt beside her and reached a hesitant, quivering hand toward her cheek.

Daphne was paralyzed. She couldn't move, and her chest had begun to burn, her heart to ache from some pain within. She winced as the stranger's fingertips hovered over her skin, then trailed over it with ghost-light care, his face still lit by the confusion and dawning joy.

"It…it can't be…" He leaned forward, closer to Daphne's prone form, and crushed his warm lips against hers, his tongue invading her mouth.

That did it—Daphne's stasis snapped and her lungs found their strength. With as much force as she could muster, she *screamed.*

"HELP!"

The young man recoiled, then moved in again, one hand covering Daphne's mouth to stifle her screams. "Be silent!" He looked around, his head turning in quick jerks as he scanned the nearby area.

Hell no.

Daphne brought her left knee up as hard as she could, slamming into her assailant's temple. He stumbled off of her, grasping the side of his head, the expression on his face a mixture of confusion and irritation. A clump of grass torn from the lawn followed the blow, splashing into his eyes, forcing him to wipe the soil away.

Daphne stood, her knees shaky, and kept screaming. Flashlights began to dart in their direction, bobbing up and down as their wielders ran towards the sound. The stranger glanced in their direction, then back the way he came.

"Daphne, stop." His words were angry, a snarl.

The shock cut off her next scream. "How…how do you know my name?"

Whistles blew as security officers came within sight. The man turned and scowled, then closed his eyes.

"Look to see me no more, but I will find you again."

Daphne's head was spinning; her thoughts a whirlpool of syllables and images, unable to coalesce into a cohesive train. "Wh...who...?"

The security was within 20 feet now; they were calling for the stranger to put up his hands, which he did. His face was set, hard, and he never took his eyes off of Daphne's.

"I will find you." A flash of light erupted, a geyser of radiance, and Daphne screamed as her eyelids clamped down to shield her from the brilliance. She could hear the officers cry out as well as they were thrown to the ground, arms over their faces.

It took several moments before the ghost lights in Daphne's vision cleared enough to see what was going on around her. In the ambient light, she noticed two things at once.

First, the strange man was gone.

Second, for about five feet around where he had stood, the grass was gone and the ground was bleached white, as if the dirt had been left in the sun too long.

Chapter Six

"And you have no idea who it was?" Chloe sat back down in her comfy chair, handing Daphne a Pepsi as she spoke. The loud music and celebration from the party could still be heard across the campus, but neither of them paid any attention. "None at all?"

Daphne sighed. "I've never seen him before." She dragged her fingertips across the moist aluminum can and licked her lips. "At least, not in real life."

Chloe almost choked on her drink; after several coughs, she turned watery eyes on her roommate. "What the hell do you mean, 'not in real life?'"

"Well..." Daphne was reluctant to speak. *How do I tell someone something like this without sounding like a lunatic?* "I've...I've dreamt about him before."

Chloe's eyes narrowed and she leaned forward in her chair. "What do you mean, dreamt about him? Are you sure it was him? What kind of dreams were these?"

"Weird. Fragmented." Daphne ran her hands through her hair and took a sip of her soda. "He was chasing me in the first one. I was terrified of him, hated him. Ran from him, but he was catching up. The look on his face..." She shuddered. "He was like an animal, Chloe. Like he was going to throw me down on the ground and fuck my brains out, no matter what I thought."

"Did he catch you?"

Daphne rubbed her temples with one hand and closed her eyes as she tried to recall the exact images from a week ago. "Yes...and no. It was strange; I couldn't move. I couldn't see him anymore. I don't think I was even breathing, but I could hear him. He ran his hands over my arm..." She swallowed another gulp of Pepsi. "...and then he bent it backwards and snapped it."

Chloe's eyes were wide as DVDs as she listened to Daphne recounting her story; at that statement, though, she recoiled. "He...he snapped your arm?"

Daphne sighed and nodded. She was tired, her head ached, and the caffeine didn't seem to be helping quickly enough. "Yeah. That's when I woke up, just as my dad pulled the car up to the parking lot."

"...and you haven't had any dreams since?"

"Not like that." She laughed. "God, I try to go to my first college party and I get waylaid by some rapist. What does *that* say about the future?"

Chloe pursed her lips, then nodded. "Maybe you should ask Cassandra."

The two exchanged glances, then Daphne chucked a pillow at her friend, slamming into her face. "No, thank you."

A moment of silence, and the levity faded. "But what about that light? The white circle? How did he do that?"

Chloe snickered, which caused Daphne to level a glare.

"Whoa, I'm sorry, but..." Another laugh. "I'm no Chemistry major, but I'm sure there's some sort of concoction or something that he could have used to do that. Doesn't magnesium burn really bright?"

Daphne's angry face began to crumble. "Well...but..."

"But nothing. Ever seen one of those street magicians?" She didn't wait for an answer. "I have. They do crazy shit, right in front of you. This doesn't sound like anything much crazier than making it look like you're flying, or that you're shoving a needle through your arm."

Daphne cracked. A small smile appeared, toying with the corners of her mouth, and she cast a sheepish look at Chloe. "Am I just overreacting?"

"Hell no! If that happened to me, I'd be freaking out too! Just...remember, we're not back in the 13th Century or whatever. Everything has a rational explanation, even if we don't know what it is at the time."

Daphne sat back in her chair. Tears were beginning to form in her eyes as the emotions roiling in her heart settled into something recognizable rather than the tempest they had been. "You're right. Of course you're right. I guess..." She laughed. "I guess my imagination was running away with me, what with Cassandra and all, and now this." She reached out and put a hand on Chloe's. "Thanks, by the way, for coming by so fast. What made you leave the party?"

"Meh." Chloe flipped her hair back over her shoulder. "No hot guys that weren't already taken, and the music sucked." A wicked smile. "Besides, I'd *much* rather listen to your stories of encounters laden with sexual tension on the college lawn."

"Hmm..." A sly look crossed Daphne's face, and she rolled her chair over to her desk and grabbed her notepad and pen. "Might make a good book idea, actually."

Chloe chuckled. "Atta girl." She glanced at her smartphone. "Hey, someone's asking if I have the study notes for Monday's exam. Are you gonna be all right?"

Daphne smiled and stood up. "I think I'll be fine, Chloe. Thanks."

Her roommate stepped forward and wrapped Daphne in a hug. "Hey, don't worry about it, girl. That's what friends are for." She gripped Daphne's shoulders and held her back to look into the girl's face. "But you need to make sure you let me know if you see this guy again. He sounds cute." As Daphne gasped, Chloe threw her head back and laughed, pushing the redhead away.

After the embrace, Daphne nudged Chloe toward the door. "All right, get going to your 'study group.' Out of curiosity..." She tapped one finger against her lips and cocked her hip to the side. "How many people are going to be *at* this study group...and how many genders?"

Chloe tried her best to look innocent. "What? Are you suggesting that I would call a date a study group session?" No response. "Fine. There'll be three of us there, total. All right?"

"...and?"

"And one of them is a girl. Okay? Satisfied?"

"I suppose. Have fun." Daphne started to turn back toward her desk.

"...Of course, that's because I think threesomes are more fun with just one guy!"

"Chloe!" Daphne's eyes widened and her cheeks went red as she pivoted her chair back toward her roommate, but Chloe had escaped, closing the door behind her with a giggle.

"Crazy girl." Daphne tried to frown, but couldn't help grinning. She put pen to paper and began to write.

"The dreams had filled her with a mixture of horror and worry for weeks, yet there was also a sense of anticipation, a part of her that wished it would come true..."

~~~

For hours, the small room had been filled with the scritches and scratches of pen on paper as Daphne worked. The images burned in her mind, and the ideas screamed to get out. She had not stood, had not stretched, had not reached over to the small fridge to grab a drink or a snack. All that mattered, all that consumed her, was the expression of this story, this tale that had invaded her and now demanded extirpation.

She did not know how long she had been writing when she paused, flexing the fingers of her right
~~~

hand to expel some of the fatigue which had built up, but the height of the moon outside shocked her.

How much have I...

She flipped back through her scrawled text, page after page. Over thirty pages had been filled in, margin to margin, in cramped, hurried writing.

"Damn." She pulled out her phone to check the time. "What the hell happened? I've never felt that before. It's almost like..."

Now that she was no longer focused on her work, she realized how hot her room was. Sweat had beaded on her forehead, her lip, the hollow between her breasts and the small of her back. She checked the air conditioner, but no setting would turn it on.

"Naturally." Daphne picked up the phone and dialed the number for the R.A. Two rings later, and the familiar voice picked up.

"Hello? What is it?"

Daphne flinched at the girl's tone. "You sound tired."

"I've been fielding calls for the last two hours about the A/C," came the reply. "Is that what you're calling about, too? I'm sorry, but there's nothing I can do about it. Maintenance says that they'll come out in the morning. Apparently, since it's nighttime, 'nobody is going to die of overheating at night.'"

Daphne opened the refrigerator and brought out a Pepsi, pressing the cold can to her forehead and neck. "I don't know about that. It's really hot tonight."

"That's what I said! We're in Florida, for God's sake! Humidity of 90% plus on a regular basis! Anyway," her voice calmed and became more subdued, "I'm sorry about the A/C. All I can recommend is for you to turn on your room fan and open your window. That should, at least, keep you from broiling in your sleep."

"Okay, Sayaka. Thanks." Daphne hung up the phone and replaced it in its cradle, then looked toward the window.

Well, guess that's the best I can do. Daphne wiped more sweat from her face as she flipped the fan on from the wall switch. The blades kicked on with the characteristic *hum* of the motor, and a breeze whipped round the room, causing Daphne to sigh in relief.

"Still too hot, though." She moved to the window, pulling on the front of her shirt to move air through it as she walked, then opened the blinds to crack the glass. As she leaned forward, something on the lawn caught her eye. She looked closer, cupping her hands around her eyes as she pressed her face into the windowpane to block out the light from her room.

"Oh, God."

He was standing in the grass outside of Weaver Hall. The grin that emerged when he caught sight of her was in sharp contrast to her memories of his angry, violent face. He beckoned her down, his eyes roving her silhouette as she stood at the window.

She could see him clearly, despite the darkness; he seemed to stand out from it, almost as if he generated his own light. There was no doubt as to what he wanted. *Come down*, the gesture said. *Come to me.*

"Crazy mother fucker." Daphne reached into her pocket for her phone. As it began ringing and she brought it to her ear, the stranger's face bunched into a grimace and he began shaking his head and waving his hands, taking a step forward as he did so.

No. Stop.

"Hello?" Chloe's voice came over the line.

"Chloe?"

"Daphne? What's wrong, girl? You sound freaked!"

"He's here." The words came out in a rush. "Right outside our dorm. Standing in the grass."

"Oh, shit." Daphne heard murmurs in the background on her roommate's end of the call, then Chloe came back strong. "Don't leave the room, okay? I'm coming home. Just try to keep an eye on him."

Daphne's eyes were still locked on to the stranger. "Okay. I'll try. This is really freaking me out, Chloe. What if he tries to get up here?"

"Is the door locked?"

Daphne glanced over to the entrance; the deadbolt was engaged. "Yeah, it..."

She returned her gaze to the grass.

The man had vanished.

"What the hell? He's gone."

"Gone? Goddamn it!" A string of curses flew from Chloe's lips; Daphne pulled the phone away from her ear to avoid having it scorched off by the strength of the expletives. When they subsided, she brought the device back.

"Um...what's wrong?"

'Oh, I'm sorry." Chloe sounded like she was between crying and screaming, but her voice was beginning to normalize. "I was just hoping to get a look at him, you know? Make sure you're not just hallucinating this guy, since he seems to keep disappearing anytime someone else could see him."

"I am not! He was there, Chloe! He was..." Daphne squinted her eyes and looked out the window once more.

Standing in the oval of light surrounding one of the campus streetlights stood someone else. A young woman. With dark hair and, upon close inspection, very light eyes.

Eyes that were staring at the spot where the man had stood.

Eyes that, then, turned to stare at Daphne, silhouetted in her window.

Eyes that might be white.

Cassandra.

"Cassandra is out there. She was watching the whole time, I think." Daphne's voice was a strained whisper as she tried hard to keep her eyes on the girl in the night, fighting the urge to run and hide from that blank, pupil-less stare.

"Cassandra? What...wait." A moment paused. "Maybe that crazy bitch has something to do with it. Maybe they're working together to kidnap you or something, you know?"

"Maybe."

Cassandra waved, once, toward Daphne, then turned and walked back toward the entrance to the Hall. "Or maybe it's just coincidence. Maybe she was out doing some sort of science experiment."

"Well, whatever she's doing there, it's getting creepy." Metal rattled on the other end of the phone. "I'm already on my way back, so I'll see you in about 20 minutes or so. Like I said, keep the door locked, don't let anyone in. I've got my key, so don't worry. I'll see you in a few, okay?"

Daphne forced herself to nod. "Okay, Chloe. I'll see you soon. Drive safe."

"I will."

The phone went dead. Daphne hung her head and held it in her hands as she sank into her room-mate's plush chair.

What is going on? She tried to calm her breathing. *Who the hell* is *this guy? What does he want from me?*

The stress and fatigue of the day pounced like a panther. Daphne felt waves of sleepiness pulling her eyes shut and muddling her thoughts, trying to drag her down into the gentle embrace of Morpheus. She resisted.

Shaking her head, she tried to keep her eyes open. She reached out for a book, a magazine, something, but before her hand could find one, her conscious mind lost its battle, and she slipped into nothingness as she sat in the plushy chair, her blue eyes veiled, one arm outstretched, and the other resting in her lap.

~~~

Daphne. Wait. Don't run.

The forest was filled with mist, and it washed over her skin with its moisture, pinpricks of cold against the flush within her. Bare feet pounded against the ground, stepping on roots, grass, and dirt alike without care or concern, yet she was not tired, was not hurt.

He was getting closer. Daphne. Stop.

A glance back was dangerous, she knew. Running this fast, looking behind you and you could tumble
~~~

head over heels as you snagged a foot or stepped into an unexpected burrow.

She did it anyway.

The strange man was following her, yes, running after her as he had done before...but something was different.

His face.

It no longer held that lust, that passion he had worn as he pursued her; instead, concern, fear, near panic were writ large upon his brow, and his hands, the slender, practiced hands of a musician or a surgeon, reached for her. Across his back was a bow, golden and magnificent.

Behind him, Daphne could see the trees moving in the mist, hear branches snapping under the weight of something running, something large.

Stop. *He pointed toward her.* Pull it out.

Pull it out?

Daphne looked down at herself. Blood coated her shirt, coated her skirt, coated her legs. A thick rivulet ran from her chest and dripped from her breasts, her fingers.

Ran from the arrow buried in her heart.

Daphne looked up at the man, who had reached her, who was ignoring the approaching calamity behind him, the calamity knocking trees aside like matchsticks.

Pull it out, Daphne. *His eyes locked onto hers, his hand moving to caress her chin.* Please.

His touch burned her skin, and she suppressed a scream.

Chapter Seven

Daphne blinked as the sun shone in her window. Her mouth tasted of sleep-funk, and a clear puddle of drool stained her shoulder. Her glasses had fallen from her face and landed on the floor beside her chair. Her lips smacked as she wrestled herself from the entangling threads of her dream, her memory out-of-focus for several seconds before she was able to get her bearings.

"Good morning, sleepyhead."

"Huh?" Daphne's hand patted the floor a few times before happening upon her glasses. "What...how long have I been asleep?"

"Well, I'm not sure." Chloe was, as usual, dressed in pajamas—today seemed to be her

Dalmatians set—and was mixing together a couple of instant oatmeal packets. "That depends on when you fell asleep."

"I...I'm not sure." She looked around the room for a few moments, trying to muster the strength to haul herself out of the chair she had, it seemed, slept in all night. "I guess a couple of minutes after I got off the phone with you."

Chloe whistled as she poured milk into her bowl. "Damn. I was a little later than I thought cause I was picking up some crisis supplies." She returned the milk to the refrigerator and opened the freezer compartment, revealing two quarts of rocky road ice cream. "By the way, I hope that chocolate is okay for you? You're not one of those weird people who prefers strawberry or anything, are you?"

Daphne managed a laugh as she pulled herself up and stumbled to the bathroom. "Chocolate's fine. So how long? What time is it?"

"Well...you called at about 2, and it's just after noon now, so..."

Daphne stopped in her tracks. "10 hours? I've been asleep 10 hours? What about class? What about..."

Chloe snickered behind her hand. "Hey, chill out, it's Saturday. We skipped the party, but I guess I can forgive you since it would have sucked anyway."

Daphne shook her head, reaching through the fog in her mind, then her eyes widened.

"Shit...Chloe! He knows where I live! He knows which room I'm in!" She rubbed her face with her hands. "I...do I need to switch rooms? Get out of here? Go back home? What if he's some murdering maniac who's waiting for the right time to get me?"

Chloe took her roommate by the shoulders. "Chill. Seriously. Chill the fuck out, Daphne. I love you and all, but these hysterics are starting to get to me."

Daphne recoiled from Chloe's admonishment. "What the hell?"

"Look. You're stressed. You're seeing stuff that isn't really happening. You fell asleep, like, right after you called me, and you had just been in a super stressful situation. You probably hallucinated the guy the second time, or thought you saw him when you didn't."

Daphne took two steps back. "You...you think I'm crazy?"

Chloe's stern look melted and she *tsked* with her tongue. "No, sweetie. I think that you're human. People under stress see all *sorts* of things that aren't really there, or they interpret them in the wrong way. Look at your day for a minute." The blonde cleared a space on the counter and dug around in her bookbag for a moment, pulling out a small stuffed girl doll with long black hair.

"Imagine this is you." The doll did a little hop in place. "So, you're almost late to the party, and that's got you freaked out." Chloe mimed the doll running along the countertop. "Suddenly, you trip, fall—maybe bang your head—and there's this guy who seems like he looks just like the guy in your dream." She tossed the doll into the air, and it landed on its back.

"Then he disappears." The doll covered its eyes with its hands. "You're interrogated at the security office." The doll sat, with its hands between its legs and its head down. "Then you come back, and you're relating the entire situation to your best friend on the phone." The doll held one of its hands to where its ear would be and paced back and forth.

"Now, down below is a guy who kinda resembles the crazy man who knocked you over." A moment of rummaging revealed a similar doll with short brown hair, who Chloe placed on the floor near the counter. "You look out, and he seems like he's looking up at your window." The girl doll toddled over to the edge of the counter. "Wouldn't it be easy for you to misinterpret what's going on? Imagine something that isn't there? Maybe the guy is looking at a nearby window; there's enough of them. Maybe he's just staring off into space." The doll flopped down as Chloe released it to put her hand on Daphne's shoulder.

"I'm telling you this as your friend. You're under a lot, a *lot* of stress, what with the change from your parents, your classes, everything. These are classic symptoms. You just need…What?"

During Chloe's entire performance, Daphne had been holding back laughter. The absurdity of the situation, combined with the cuteness of the little puppet show before her, had struck her as *hilarious*. Her eyes were closed and leaking tears, and her face was twisted up like someone who had just bitten into a lemon. At her roommate's question, though, the dam broke and the room was flooded by her howls of laughter. Deep, hooting gasps of amusement drowned out the sound of Daphne's hand pounding against the chair as she held onto it for support with the other.

Chloe's brow wrinkled and she leaned in closer to Daphne. "Are…are you okay?"

Daphne tried to respond, but her gasps were only broken by more laughter. "I…I…" A glance into Chloe's concerned face set off another bout of howling. The blonde girl stared a moment longer, then shook her head and, smiling, sat down in her chair to wait out the storm.

"You should have seen your face." Daphne's words were broken, her breath still coming in gasps. "You were…so serious…with that doll!" The memory only increased Daphne's hysterics.

"Okay, okay." Chloe shrugged but her smile had not left. "Knock it off. You'll have the neighbors calling the cops, thinking you've gone crazy."

A few minutes passed as the peals of laughter subsided to chuckles, then chortles, then occasional titters. Daphne had wrapped her arms around her stomach and was wincing at the pain in her sides. Her breath was a staccato of rapid wheezes, and tears streaked her cheeks.

"Are you done?"

Daphne nodded, suppressing another laugh. "I'm sorry...but it was *really* funny."

Chloe's smile still held, but it seemed stretched, thin. "Glad I could amuse you. Look, I've got some things I need to take care of today so I probably won't be in until late." Before Daphne could respond, Chloe grabbed some clothes from her bed and dashed out of the room.

"Great job." Daphne hit her forehead with the heel of her hand. "Run off my one good friend here because I can't keep my laughter to myself." She caught a look at herself in the mirror and grimaced.

Better get a shower. Daphne sighed, turned, and walked toward the bathroom. *Then I guess I'll go find somewhere to do some homework.*

Her stomach grumbled, and she smiled. *...And something to eat.*

Chapter Eight

The midday sunlight dappled on the trimmed grass in front of the Library West building. Students walked in and out, passing under the arched doorways to do research or check out books. Others sat in the yard, reading, listening to music, talking to friends, or just relaxing.

Daphne was curled up under a tree with her Kindle, sheltered from the direct heat of the day. Her take-out box lay open, the burrito and most of the chips missing. She was enraptured by Greek myths; in the last hour, she had devoured stories about Hercules' labors and the tale of Sisyphus, condemned to roll a boulder up a hill for eternity.

She swiped to the next page. A new chapter with the heading *Clytie and Apollo* brought her out of her reading-trance and back to reality.

Damn. She stared off, remembering her room-mate's face as she had been confronted with Daphne's laughter. *I need to make that up to her...I didn't mean to hurt her feelings.* Another several moments passed and the girl sighed, put her tablet back in her bag, and hoisted herself to her feet.

A smile broke its way through the gloom that had attached itself. "Popcorn! I bet she would really like some popcorn and a movie tonight!" Decision made, Daphne picked up the remnants of her meal and set off toward the Publix most students used for groceries.

As she passed the library entrance, a brunette with white eyes tracked her path.

~~~

As usual on the weekend, the Publix was filled with students looking for ways to spend their financial aid. As she made her way to the dry snacks section, Daphne waved to a couple of people she recognized from her classes.

"Popcorn...popcorn...Ah! Here we go!" Daphne bypassed the bags of instant popcorn and grabbed a container of kernels. "Always tastes better home-made, but I'm going to need butter and salt, too." She looked around, browsing and glancing at various foodstuffs as she rounded the corner.

Her foot landed on soft grass.
~~~

Daphne's eyes widened and she jumped back, dropping the Orville Redenbacher's as her gaze darted to and fro like a frightened deer. Where there had been shelves filled with chips and juice, there now stood great oaks and pines; tiled floors and ceiling had been replaced with grass and sticks, and a canopy concealing open sky.

"What...the...hell?" Her heart began racing and it became hard to catch her breath. She sank to the ground, hyperventilating. "Where are my shoes? What is going on?"

The sounds of birds singing floated over the wind drifting through the treetops and rustling the leaves. Daphne could hear, mixed with the sound of her breath, the bubbling of water nearby. She closed her eyes.

"This is a dream." She rocked back and forth and curled her legs up into her chest. "This is a dream, I'm going to wake up, this is a dream..."

She peeked one eye open.

The forest remained, despite her best efforts to disbelieve it.

Daphne remained there, curled up, for several minutes, but when nothing else seemed to happen—no stranger chasing her, no arrow buried in her chest—and her heart had slowed enough, she stood on wobbly legs and began pushing her way through the forest toward the babbling sound.

The ground was gentle on her feet, the grass seeming to bend so as not to prick her and the soil curving to cushion her step. High in the sky, far off, a great mountain towered over the landscape, its pinnacle wreathed in clouds and fog. The breeze was sweet and fragrant, and the sunlight drifting through the boughs danced on her skin like warm pixie toes. As she stepped forward, low-lying branches brushed her clothing with soft caresses before opening into a clearing that surrounded a gentle spring.

The spring flowed forth from a rock into a great pool, crystal-clear and sparkling with reflected sunlight. Does and bucks approached the water, sipping from it before bounding off into the greenery again. Daphne looked around, her fear lost in the beauty she was witnessing.

A leaf from a nearby branch flicked across her face and drew her attention upwards. The color drained from her skin and her hands flew to her mouth as she saw thousands, millions of snakes—constrictors, cobras, rattlesnakes—of all sizes climbing, impossibly climbing, in the treetops. The canopy was thick with them.

It wasn't the wind at all, was it? It was them.

The snakes hissed and twisted, and Daphne stepped backward, further into the clearing. The sight was so terrifying, so transfixing, that she could not look away despite her horror.

They aren't coming in. A few more moments' observation confirmed her suspicion. *I don't think they can come into the clearing.*

This should have been comforting, but Daphne still moved, backing away into the center.

"They won't hurt you," a soft, flowing voice whispered from behind her. Daphne's heart ramped up again as she leapt out of her skin; for just a moment, her vision wavered and she lost track of her limbs.

No! You will NOT faint!

The blackness encroaching on the edge of her vision retreated and she regained her fingers and toes. Trying to slow her rapid inhalations, she took a deep breath and turned around.

There was no one there.

"Great." She put a hand on her chest, over her heart. "I'm going even *more* insane."

"No." The voice came from below. "Down here."

Daphne's gaze found the spring; below the surface and camouflaged by the rippling waves was a naked form. It resembled a woman, with long, flowing hair and sea-green eyes, but her skin was translucent and faded in and out of the water; as she rose up and her head broke the surface, it was impossible to tell if the fluid cascading down her body was water on her skin, or *her skin itself.*

Something *snapped* in Daphne's mind. *Okay. Sure. Whatever.*

Daphne held up her hand. "Look, I'm having a real weird day. I've come closer to fainting three times in the last five minutes than I have the rest of my life, so don't be too hard on me." She looked around, gesturing to the clearing, the forest, the snakes, the mountain...

"What the hell is going on?"

The figure was now halfway out of the water, and the fact that she was wearing no clothes to cover her curves tickled Daphne's brain, but the situation she had found herself in was too insane to worry about such niceties for long.

"You slipped through the cracks." The water creature smiled. "Part of you must still remember what it was like to be one of us...or maybe it's because you met *him*."

"One of...what? Met who?" Daphne put the heels of her hands to her eyes. "Look, I just want to go home, wake up in my bed, let this all be some crazy nightmare and get everything going back to being *normal*. Is that all right? Can we do that?"

The water girl's smile drooped; her eyes narrowed, then flicked to a point over Daphne's shoulder.

"Very well. Sleep now, Sister Daphne. I hope I will see you soon."

"Wait." Daphne began to turn to see what the creature had looked at. "What's..."

~~~

Daphne's eyes were covered in cloth, and it was hard to breathe. Her limbs were trapped and bound up by the same material. She inhaled to scream.

"Whoa, whoa," came a familiar voice. "How'd you get *this* tangled, anyway?"

The scream died in Daphne's throat. The voice belonged to Chloe, her roommate; the fabric she was trapped in was her bedsheets, wrapped about her several times as if she had been tossing and turning all night long. Her eye peeked out to see the amused face of her friend.

"Umm...help?"

"That's what I'm trying to do, crazy-pants!" A few minutes of tugging, twisting, and giggling later, Daphne was released from her bedding-bondage and sitting on the ground surrounded by sheets.

"You must have been having one hell of a dream!" Chloe was dressed in a short sports coat and tight-fitting jeans, a departure from her usual pajamas while in her room. "Why are you taking a nap in the middle of the day, anyway? Has this 'weird-guy-thing' got you that tired?"

"Yeah..." Daphne shook her head. "I think you might have been right, Chloe; I think that I might be going crazy!" Tears welled up in her eyes.
~~~

"What do you mean?" Chloe leaned forward to take Daphne's hands into her own. Her gaze dug deep. "Did something happen? Tell me!"

Daphne was taken aback for a moment by Chloe's piercing look and the ardor behind her voice, but she continued. "Well...I was at Publix, after you...after I did my studying, and I thought, 'Hey, why don't I get us some popcorn and a movie so we can have a nice evening?' I turn a corner and suddenly I'm in this forest and there are trees and a giant mountain and snakes in the trees and a clearing with a water nymph or something and then I was here."

Daphne inhaled.

Chloe gaped."You...you got...what, teleported?"

Daphne's crying got worse. "That's just it! I don't know anymore!" She got up and went over to her desk, rummaging in one of the drawers. "I...I think I need to call my family, get them to come pick me up. I need some sort of help or something." Her hand touched her cell and removed it from the desk.

"No!" Chloe leapt to her feet and reached to take Daphne's phone from her hand. Daphne didn't move fast enough.

"Hey! What...what are you doing?" Daphne lunged for the device, but Chloe held her off with her other hand. The ensuing game of "Keep-Away" lasted for about two minutes before Daphne stopped trying to regain her phone.

"You don't need to leave." Chloe's breath was a little heavy. "Look, I know that this is freaking you out and all...but I think it's really exciting!" Her eyes lit up and she smiled at Daphne.

"E...exciting? What do you mean? I'm *losing* my *mind*; how is that *exciting?*"

Chloe shook her head and waved her hands in front of her. "No, no. You're not losing your mind. I think that what is happening to you is...well, that it's connected to God."

Daphne blinked. *I don't know what I was expecting her to say, but it wasn't* that.

Chloe nodded. "Level with me for a minute. You keep seeing this very handsome young man who appears and then vanishes, and no one else sees him, right? Then, you're brought into a beautiful garden, idyllic, with snakes that can't get in? Doesn't that sound like the Garden of Eden to you?"

Daphne felt like she was falling behind in a race. "Wait...you're saying...that God is doing this to me?"

Chloe's eyes were burning, bright and fervent. "He works in mysterious ways, Daphne. Maybe He's trying to show you something, or tell you something. Maybe you're a bigger part of His plan than you thought."

"Ummm..." Daphne glanced right then left. "Well, I guess that could be it...maybe."

"Just don't go." Chloe grasped Daphne's hand. "Please. Not yet. If something else crazy happens and it doesn't feel like God to you, then fine, I understand. But please, I don't want to miss this chance."

Great, now I find out my roommate is one of those crazy Jesus-freaks. Daphne stretched her lips into a smile and nodded. Chloe clapped her hands and bounded toward the door.

"Everything's going to be fine! You'll see!" She vanished, leaving Daphne alone in the quiet room. After several moments, she jumped up and poked her head out of the doorway, looking left, then right.

Chloe was nowhere in sight.

"Thank God." Daphne opened her closet door and drew out a suitcase, then started throwing in the essentials—some clothes, toothbrush and toothpaste, her Kindle.

"Okay." The plan was to get to the bus station and book a Greyhound, then call her parents and let them know she was on her way. "Got everything. Now it's time to..."

She turned around, and her hands went numb. She dropped the bag she had just packed.

He was there.

In her room.

Not five feet from her.

This was the first time she had gotten to see him in full light, without strange goings-on interfering with her concentration. His skin was a gentle olive, untouched by blemish or wrinkle. Golden ringlets tumbled down around his shoulders, and his green eyes were as deep as the forests they resembled. His jaw was strong, and his muscular frame filled out his t-shirt and jeans.

Daphne felt that familiar burning in her heart.

The man's eyes danced like those of a child who had been caught in the act, doing something that he was not supposed to do and too proud of it to deny the truth. He slowly moved his hands in front of his waist, hands open and palms up, and dared a tiny smile.

"...Can we speak now, Daphne?"

His voice was rich, smooth, masculinity distilled into liquid form and poured into her ears. She felt her heart begin to race...and the burning increased, going from a minor case of heartburn to a roaring fire in seconds, driving her to the ground whimpering and clenching her chest.

The stranger dropped with her, his hands reaching out for her but stopping an inch or so before touching her skin. "Are you all right?"

The burning began to fade as Daphne made deliberate attempts to breathe. She closed her eyes and inhaled through her nose in regular, rhythmic fashion. When she reopened them, the man was still there, his eyes raking her body, his lips pursed.

"You are not ill." His brow was furrowed in concentration. "But you are in distress. I suppose this should come as no surprise. Yet your presence, your very existence, was unforeseen. This introduces dangerous uncertainties into the situation, so I must investigate." His gaze returned to her face. "Can you, will you, sit? I believe it is safe, for now, but I can never be sure how long safety will last."

Daphne stood for a moment, the shock still evident in her system, before her mind seized control. *Damn it. Get a hold of yourself.*

"I'll stand, thank you." Daphne crossed her arms and leaned back in classically protective body language; the stranger nodded with a small upturn of his lip, then took a seat. His t-shirt clung to the muscles of his shoulders and chest, and Daphne found her eyes drawn to the carved stone which appeared to be underneath.

"Who are you, then? Why are you stalking me? Why shouldn't I just call the police right now and have you taken to jail?"

The man leaned forward, crossing his hands and twisting the fingers together as he spoke. "These are all good questions. Let us begin at the end: you should not call the police because to do so would be to place my life and existence in great danger."

Daphne cocked an eyebrow. "You mean *besides* being locked up in a cell."

He nodded. "Much worse than that. It would telegraph my location to my adversaries."

He speaks like an old wizard from a fantasy novel. "Okay. Why are you stalking me?"

He sighed. "I am not...*stalking* you. I...we..." A flush came to his cheeks and he bowed his head, chewing on his lips as he considered his words. "We knew each other, once, long ago, and I thought that you had been taken forever from me. When I saw you, that night when we happened upon one another, I was unable to believe it. I did not foresee your presence, and so I had to see you again."

"Why?" Despite herself, Daphne had uncrossed her arms and begun to lean forward; the man's words were not just smooth and warm, caressing her mind as he spoke, but the rhythm and tone he used was hypnotic, like a sorcerer weaving a spell with a story.

"To be sure it was you. To be sure that my mind had not been deceived, that my enemies had not found a way to read the depths of my heart and conjure illusions from within it." He met her eyes again. "And, I suppose, I was...nervous...about approaching you. Our first meeting was—"

Daphne's eyes darkened, and her brow knotted up in anger. "You tried to rape me."

His head fell. "I do not pretend that I was justified, but there was cause. I was overwhelmed by the sight of you, the nearness of you. I..." He trailed off, shook his head. "After that, it was harder. I knew you were angry, and I had to muster my courage each time. When you appeared in my sanctuary, I was unprepared. I did not know how to explain what you had seen, what you were experiencing, and so..."

"Wait, wait." She shook her head. "Your sanctuary? You mean...that...that weird place with the mountain and the snakes and the water nymph who knew my name?"

"Yes."

She searched his eyes, his face, for any flicker of amusement or untruth.

She found none. Her gaze dropped.

"Then it was...it was all real, wasn't it?"

He nodded. "It was. This all has been, Daphne, although I understand why you would not believe so, why your mind would rebel against the idea that such things could occur." A sad smile. "This is the result of the world you have grown up in."

His words touched a nerve, causing Daphne to look back at him. "...Did you grow up in a different world, or something? I mean, you sure talk differently, and you look..." She shook her head again. "But what do you mean? Are you really that different?"

The man nodded again. "There is much to tell you, Daphne, but I can begin with this. You are correct...I did come from a different world. In fact, my father..."

"Was much easier to find than you have been!"

Daphne's head whipped around to the entrance to the room; Chloe stood there, silhouetted in the doorway, brandishing two wicked blades. She wore all white, slacks, a shirt, and a vest, but the vest bore a large red cross embroidered over the heart. Daphne could see several other people in the hallway behind her.

The stranger stood and took a step back, and his face showed a flicker of fear. Chloe took a step forward, leveling her weapons at the man's throat.

"Chloe! What are you doing here? What...what's going on?" Daphne felt adrift, confused. Her eyes jerked from one to the other of them. "What is this?"

"This woman is here to slay me, Daphne." The stranger stepped closer to the window. "As she and her companions have done to all of my family."

"Wha...no! Chloe, you're not..." She focused on Chloe, on her roommate's face; within she saw no mercy, no gentility, no friendship, simply focused hatred leveled at the man before her.

"He is an abomination, Daphne." Chloe's voice was flat; the stranger's doom was already done, if one were to believe her tone. "He must be destroyed, for the good of the world."

The stranger barked a laugh. "Yes, because the world you have created is so much better than the one we tried to build, before you cut us down. Are these wars, these plagues, these faithless hordes what your God desired when He set you upon us? Or, perhaps, could you have overreached?" He took another step back; his shoulders pressed against the wall next to the window.

Chloe snorted. "I do not need to explain myself to you. You are a walking blasphemy, and I do service to my faith in destroying you."

Daphne threw herself between the two, facing Chloe. "No! This has got to stop! You do not just come in here and...and...threaten to *kill* someone! What has happened to you?"

Chloe moved in and tried to shove Daphne out of the way with her forearm, but the other woman held her ground. "This does not concern you, Daphne! Step out of the way. God commands it!" The figures behind Chloe began to press forward, attempting to move around her and advance on the stranger. Daphne spread her arms wide.

"I don't know what the fuck you guys think you're doing, but..."

"Thank you, Daphne."

She turned at the resonant sound of the stranger's voice. He stood next to the window, his hand on the wall beside, looking back at her. He was lit by the midday sun, the golden light shimmering on his skin and making it seem as if he were forged of the metal himself. No longer clad in a t-shirt and jeans, the man now wore ornate armor, plates of silver filigreed with golden designs of the sun, which fit him as though it were molded to his body. Outside the window, bright yellow and orange flames roiled, from a source unseen.

"No!" Chloe and the others lunged forward, knocking Daphne aside and bringing their weapons to bear. The stranger kissed his fingertips and spread them towards Daphne, then burst through the window in a shower of shattering glass. Daphne, Chloe, and the others in the room reached the window in time to see a flaming chariot, pulled by two horses born of sun-fire, streaking away into the sky.

"You fucking *bitch!*" Chloe lashed out at Daphne, backhanding her and sending her tumbling across the room. Chloe advanced on the girl. "Do you *know* what you've done?" Daphne struggled to her feet, only to be clubbed in the head by the hilt of the other girl's knife and sent down again. "Do you *know* how long it fucking took us to find him? I've been looking for centuries! And you let him get away!"

Blood began to flow from Daphne's head wound into her eyes; she looked up, blinking away the stinging, as her roommate, her face twisted and angry, reared back for another strike.

"Commander!" one of the men behind her called out.

Chloe's posture did not change. Her eyes blazed into Daphne's, and her knuckles were white around the handle of her blade.

She's going to kill me. Daphne's heart was a drum in her chest, beating to a madman's rhythm. *Oh, God, she's crazy. She's going to kill me.*

The blonde lowered her fist, but her muscles were tensed as if to do so was a great effort. Her visage remained a mask of fury as she turned back to the other men and women; as Daphne glanced toward them, she saw that they wore the same white vests with the red cross emblazoned over the heart.

Chloe's face twisted into a snarl. "He can't have dropped off the radar that easily." The followers around her drew themselves up into attention. "Using that kind of power right now is going to leave him vulnerable, and a flaming chariot is going to be easy to track. Get in contact with the Knight-Captain and let him know what happened here, Francis."

"Yes, ma'am," replied the man who had interrupted her before she could hit Daphne a third time. Although obviously athletic and fit, he was balding and looked older than Chloe. Despite his age, his posture and that of the others demonstrated that she was in command.

She turned to address the rest.

"The rest of you need to be ready to move out. As soon as we get word of a landing site, we need to be there, preferably *before* he has a chance to get his bearings. The end is in sight, soldiers. One more and we've accomplished our mission."

"*God wills it!*" cried the assembled, before they filed out of the room.

Chloe turned back to Daphne; her gaze was still angry, but, as her eyes skittered over the young woman's injuries and hurt look, something like compassion and concern stole into them.

Daphne wiped more of the blood from her face, wincing as her fingers brushed against the bruises and cuts. "God wills it? Wills *what,* exactly? Bashing your roommate in the face after trying to kill someone? Or is it lying about who and what you are?" She spat out a hunk of bloody phlegm. "Get away from me, Chloe. If that's really your name."

Chloe sighed; the anger seemed to drain from her face like water down a drain, and she plopped into her comfortable chair. "It is my name, if that's any comfort, although I imagine it's probably not. I'm sorry I hit you, Daphne. I can't really explain except to tell you that I was angry and I lost control."

"Funny." Daphne moved away, putting a little more distance between them. "But when *I* get angry and lose control I might scream or smash my fist into a table or something. I don't tend to attack people with knives and shit."

"No, I suppose not." Chloe pulled up the leg of her pants to reveal a hidden sheath, then slipped one of her blades into it. "I hope you know that I enjoyed spending time with you, even if I wasn't completely honest about everything." She laughed, but the sound was hollow. "Actually, I thought that Cassandra would be the key, the creepy girl saying she can see the future, just like he can. It wasn't until you told me about your dreams that I realized he was coming for you."

Daphne pulled her knees up into her chin. "I don't care. Go away, Chloe. Get out, or I'll call the police."

Chloe looked sidelong at Daphne, and a hint of the old anger flared in her eyes. "If I didn't want you to do that, you wouldn't, Daphne. Trust me." She reached into the inside pocket of her vest, and pulled out a bag.. "It doesn't matter anyway; in just a moment, you won't remember anything."

Daphne's face snapped up. "Wait, what?"

Chloe passed her hand over Daphne's head, sprinkling a luminescent, rainbow-shimmering crystalline powder over her. As it landed on her hair and skin, a pearlescent sheen began to spread over her body, despite her frantic attempts to brush it off.

"Taken from Hermes." She closed the bag again. "And, supposedly, extracted from the water of the Lethe River, salt from the waters of forgetfulness. All this might surface time and again in your dreams, Daphne, but you will never again remember the strange man you saw, or me. Goodbye."

Daphne struggled, even as her lips went numb, her voice left, and her limbs grew heavy. She kept struggling as darkness closed in on her mind and her vision, kept struggling as her thoughts fell off, one by one, until a solitary straggler remained, until she could no longer remember what she was struggling against, only that she must fight, must not give in, must not let go.

Until the image of the strange man, clad in solar glory and burned into her mind, finally faded away into the black.

Chapter Nine

"Uuhhhh..."

Daphne awoke, opening her eyes. The throbbing in her head begged her to recant, but she straightened up from the comatose slouch she was in, rubbing her forehead and wincing as her fingers pressed against swollen bruises.

"What...happened?" Daphne's voice was slurred, and she staggered to her feet and moved toward the bathroom. She managed to avoid tripping on any of the clothes or books that were strewn across the floor, only to slam her head into the doorframe on her way in.

"Owww..." With effort, she focused her eyes on her reflection in the mirror.

My God, what happened to me? I look like I was run over by a freight train. Her eyes were red and puffy, blood had run in rivulets and caked across the bridge of her nose, and her forehead and cheek were black and purple with pain. Her teeth felt grimy, like some sort of sand or dirt had gotten in her mouth.

Did I get wasted at that party or something? She fumbled for her phone in her pocket, pulled it out, and squinted to check the time. 10:04 in the morning, Monday.

She had lost almost three days.

"Oh God." Her voice came in a whisper, tight and tense with suppressed panic. She began examining herself, looking for any evidence of assault or rape; stories of date-rape drugs that blocked out all memories ran through her mind as she checked herself over.

There was nothing. Aside from the open wounds and swelling on her face and some bruises on her back that probably came from her fall to Earth, she couldn't find any evidence of assault. She looked back to the mirror, probed at the injuries.

"Then what the hell *happened?*" Daphne brought out her phone and started firing off texts to her classmates, acquaintances, friends: *How was your weekend? Did you make it to that party?*

She paced, trying to remember, trying to conjure up images of the last several days. Ghostly, fleeting remembrances—Cassandra's white eyes in the darkness, dolls dancing, burning white light...all blurred together until she wasn't sure if they were real at all.

Her phone buzzed, and she brought it up. Lindsey.

LINDSEY: *Hey, Daph! Where've you been? Meet someone and get sidetracked? ;)*

Daphne almost laughed as she typed in her reply. *Not hardly. Hope you had fun at the party. Gotta go, TTYL.*

A few minutes later, another response, then two more. No one mentioned her, or an accident or incident that could have caused her injuries.

"So I never made it to the party. Have I been here the whole time?" She shook her head, winced, hissed from behind her teeth. "Maybe...maybe I bumped my head? Fell down somewhere?" As she mused, Daphne walked to the window, looked out on the milling studentry. "Security would know."

She dialed the number for campus security. "Hello? Yes, I need to know if there...if I've...if..."

"If what, young lady?"

"Just...did someone named Daphne Gianakos get hurt, have to be taken to the emergency room or the hospital? Maybe bump her head?" She twirled the drapes in one hand while she talked.

"I'm sorry, but I can't discuss—"

"Look, I'm Daphne." She closed her eyes and leaned her forehead against the glass. "I think that maybe I hit my head, got a concussion or something, because I don't remember the last three days."

The officer's voice sharpened. "Were you drugged? Raped? Do you—"

"No, no, none of that. I checked. I'm fine, other than a few bumps and small cuts, except for the memory." She sighed. "Can you check on that for me? Maybe someone found me lying in the library or something, called for help? I don't know." A short, barking laugh. "Hell, maybe I did it myself and just can't remember."

"If you come in with some ID, I can check on that for you, but I don't remember anything like that coming in over the weekend." Daphne heard a tapping sound from the officer's end, a pen on a desk.

She let go of the curtain and opened her eyes. "Yeah, thanks. I'll be in when I can." The faint reflection of her face in the window stared back at her, confused, uncertain. "Thank you for your help."

Daphne sat at her desk. *Okay. If no one reported anything...then, what? Was it here? Did I fall down in my own room?* She raised her eyebrows and laughed at herself.

"God, *that's* a story to tell people, isn't it? 'How was your first year at college, Daphne?' 'Oh, not so bad, except for the time I knocked myself cold and forgot three whole days.'" Her eyes drifted to the empty bed next to hers.

Wonder if they're ever going to get me a room-mate. Might not have to ask all these questions if I had one.

Her eyes continued to roam across the room, settling on the thin blades of the laurel tree she had brought with her from home.

What the... She leaned forward to take a closer look. In a week and a half, the tree had grown two feet and was as thick around as the base of her wrist. The leaves were lush and, as Daphne observed by rubbing one between her fingers, firm and wet. A tingle came over her as she caressed the greenery, causing an involuntary shudder. A strange sense of vertigo swept over the young woman; for a moment, it was as if she could see two rooms, as if she lived in two places. Echoes of voices from one could almost be heard in the other.

Daphne shook her head to clear it. *College stress. Nothing else. Need to relax or I'm really going to lose it.* She checked the clock again—10:37. *No classes until two today. Maybe I should go decompress.* She stood. *Go see a movie.*

As Daphne closed the door on her way out, a new leaf sprouted from the laurel tree, uncurled, and joined its brethren in the glow of the Sun.

~~~
~~~

"Was Henry Cavill *hot* in that movie or what?" Susannah, a short, petite girl who had embraced the bygone Goth tradition, spun around in a small circle as the trio left the theater.

"I know! And, I mean, I liked him with that beard and all, but when it was shaved off and he was all, like, 'I'm Superman.' I swear I about fainted right there." Kaitlyn, a young Asian who preferred pastel shades, put her hand to her head in an exaggerated display of wooziness. "What about you, Daph? What was your favorite part?"

Daphne laughed. "It's a good thing I ran into you girls or you wouldn't have been able to indulge your drool-obsession with Cavill's pecs." Everyone smiled, but Daphne's disappeared as she contemplated the question.

"Well, I've always loved Superman." She adjusted her glasses on her nose. ""He's the first real superhero that anyone ever wrote about—he created the archetype."

"But he's always doing the 'right thing." Kaitlyn shook her head as Susannah nodded. "There's no...no flaw in him." She shrugged. "If he weren't being played by such a hot actor, I wouldn't give a damn about him."

"Plus, I like my superheroes a little...darker. Like Wolverine." Susannah put a hand to her forehead, miming a fainting spell. "Superman...I mean, Cavill's hot and all but he doesn't hold a candle to Hugh Jackman."

Daphne was shaking her head. "That's not it at all. Superman...well, he's pretty much the most powerful creature in that universe. Almost none of the other superheroes or supervillains compare."

"Yeah." Susannah popped another piece of popcorn in her mouth. "That's part of what makes him boring. I mean, even in the movie he never really got hurt. What's the fun in somebody who's pretty much invincible? Where's the fun in the story?"

Daphne's eyes widened. "It's all *about* the story! There is a man, almost a *god*, who could, by himself, swoop in and fix mankind's problems—no more war, no more crime, none of it."

"If he cares about us so much, then why wouldn't he do it?" Kaitlyn downed the last of her Diet Coke, tossing the cup into the trash can outside the restrooms. "Why would he let us keep killing each other and shit?"

"Free will!" Daphne threw her hands in the air in her excitement; a few passers-by gave her strange glances and hurried on their ways. "He knows that to infringe on our freedoms, our right to make those choices, those mistakes, would be a greater evil than all of the terrible crimes it would prevent. We would all be slaves, forced to act in accordance with Superman's dictates...and the fact that he chooses *not* to do that, despite the constant temptation to just make us *stop*, is just..." She paused to take a sip from her water bottle; her face was red, flushed with heat from the discussion.

"Kind of like that thing Benjamin Franklin said...what was it...?" Susannah frowned in thought. "'Those who would give up Essential Liberty to purchase a little Temporary Safety deserve neither Liberty nor Safety.'" Daphne nodded and Kaitlyn snorted.

"Sounds more like something that should be in some religion or philosophy class. 'Free will?' He's just a fictional character. Fictional characters should be bad-ass, be the kind of people we wish we could be." Kaitlyn waved her hands around in the air. "I mean, he's just like, 'Oh, look at me, I'm such a good guy that everybody tries to kill me cause I'm so good.'" She laughed.

Daphne shrugged as she pushed through the outer doors, blinking in the sudden sunlight. "I don't think you get it. The Superman story is rich with symbolism and meaning. If my characters in any of my books are half as in-depth and compelling as he is, I'll be a millionaire inside a year."

Susannah gasped. "You're writing a book? Really? What's it about?"

"Well..." Daphne's eyes drifted as her mind dredged up the storyline. "It's got dragons, and princesses, and..."

The Century Tower began to chime.

"Oh, shit, I've got to get to Theology!" Daphne adjusted her bookbag and turned to her companions. "See you in lab!"

Without waiting for a reply, Daphne dashed toward her classroom.

Chapter Ten

"In this unit, we are going to discuss the literary merits of various religious texts and writings, and describe how they conform to classic storytelling techniques." Dr. Kinkade swept the room with his dark eyes and smoothed his tie. "The first text is one that most people in the United States are at least passingly familiar with—the Holy Bible."

Daphne sat in her desk in a sea of over fifty other students. The classroom's A/C system was struggling to keep them all comfortable, but if the sounds reverberating through the vents were any indication, it was losing the battle.

At the professor's words, the customary shuffling of bookbags and laptops began as students retrieved their copies of the Good Book. Daphne placed hers on her desktop with the red cover bearing the words HOLY BIBLE on top.

"Now, let's turn to the Book of Exodus, Chapter 20. This portion of the text is known as the Ten Commandments. Can anyone tell me what they represent in religious mythology?"

A whisper came from beside Daphne. "Hey, what happened to your face?"

Daphne turned in her seat. A young man with slicked-back brown hair and a leather jacket was leaning forward, eyebrows up, worry writ on his face. She licked her lips. "...Fell in the shower, John. Shh."

John retreated into his seat just in time to avoid the piercing glare of Dr. Kinkade. After a second or two of awkward silence, the professor resumed his lecture. "Exactly. This served as a method for the God of the Hebrews to control the actions of his worshipers." He paused a moment, clearing his throat before taking a sip from his water bottle. "Can anyone tell me one major difference between the laws set forth for the Jews, and those of other religions that existed at the same time and came later?"

Papers shuffled and low murmurs spread through the assembled studentry, but no one spoke up. Kinkade nodded, his mien unchanged.

"While there were other monotheistic religions, Judaism is the only purely monotheistic faith to survive in any significant numbers into today. In fact,

Judaism could be seen as the progenitor of at least two other major monotheistic faiths—Christianity and Islam, and all the sects thereof." Another sip of water. "Both of these belief systems acknowledge that the Old Testament is, at least mostly, correct, although they may interpret it differently.

"Now, if you'll..."

The rest of the professor's lesson blurred in Daphne's mind, PowerPoint slides merging with the rising and falling cadence of his voice. *Nobody mentioned anything, other than John.* She glanced around the room, but everyone else seemed to be either attentive or trying to hide the fact that they weren't. *Must be that no one saw it, whatever happened. If I had been dancing on a table and fell down, people'd be talking about it.*

Dr. Kinkade glanced up at the clock. "For homework, by Wednesday I want you to have written out the Ten Commandments and what the implications of those rules have been, both historically and in the modern day." He tapped the side of his nose. "Make sure to cite your sources."

Mumbles and groans ensued as students jotted down the assignment in their planners and tablets. Daphne closed her Bible and shoved it back into her bag, shouldered it, and headed out the door. As she crossed the threshold, she felt something land on her shoulder.

"Aaahh!" She turned about, heart pumping like a medieval fireman at the well. "Damn it, John!" Daphne held her hand over her heart and tried to calm her breathing.

"Sorry. I was just..." The young man stepped aside to let more people exit the classroom, rubbing the back of his neck as he spoke, and glanced around. "I just wanted to make sure you were okay." He gestured to the wounds on her face again. "Those don't look like you fell in the shower. They look like someone punched you." A moment of hesitation. "A lot."

Daphne winced, looking down as she felt his eyes probing her injuries. "Thanks, John, but I'm fine. Nobody punched me in the face. I seriously fell." She laughed. "Probably looked like an idiot, too."

John examined her for a few seconds more, then nodded. "Okay." He licked his lips and smiled. "Then, how about we go out...for some ice cream or something? Tonight? Or tomorrow?"

Daphne opened her mouth to respond, but an image interrupted her train of thought: green eyes, the skin around them crinkled in a smile, locked onto hers. Full lips pursed in thought, then shaping words, teeth flashing as they moved. A white t-shirt, stretched over—

"Daphne? Hello? Earth to Daphne?!" John was waving his hand in front of her face. Daphne's mouth snapped shut, and she swallowed to clear the cotton from her throat.

"God...how long have I been standing here?" Her flushed face belied her laughing, self-deprecating tone.

John sighed, then chuckled. "About a minute. I was starting to get worried. First, I thought you were just so shocked by my offer that you couldn't think of anything to say, but when you started to drool I was concerned." He glanced around, then turned back to Daphne.

"...Was it a seizure? Petit mal?" She stared at him for a moment, but he paid no mind. "I get those sometimes—well..." He made a rocking, "so-so" motion with his hand. "I haven't gotten one in almost a year now, so I'm hoping that I've finally outgrown them."

Daphne chewed her bottom lip before responding. "...Yeah. That's what it was. I didn't want people to know because it always seems like they think I'm a freak or something."

"I know, right? No matter how many times I tried to explain that it's just a misfiring brain-thing, they still stared at me whenever they passed by in the hallway at school." John smiled again and patted Daphne on the shoulder, then took a scrap of paper from his wallet and jotted something down.

"Here's my number." He handed the slip to Daphne, avoiding eye contact as he did so. "If you decide that you're up for a little ice cream or whatever, let me know, okay? No pressure."

Daphne took the scrap and moved in to give John a hug. "Thanks," she added as she moved out of the embrace, "but don't expect anything. I've got homework and lots of other things on my mind." She took off her glasses and rubbed the lenses clean with the hem of her shirt. "I'll see you around, okay?"

John's smile remained, although the smile around his eyes had vanished. "Yep, I'll see you in class, I guess. Take care of yourself." He turned and walked away, leaving Daphne staring at his back until he vanished.

Why did you turn him down? She hurried out of the building and toward her English class. *What is your major malfunction, Daph?*

"I don't know." Her thoughts began to vocalize in low mumbles as she walked. "It just...just didn't feel right." She turned a corner, merging into a main cross-campus pathway. "Maybe it was that I had just lied to him about the whole seizure thing. I don't know."

Daphne looked up; shock spread across her face as she realized she had entered her classroom. Her professor was setting up his lecture equipment, and students were getting out their books and preparing to take notes.

Excerpt from Cassandra's Diary—August 29th

The Golden Man flees west, following the sun on its path as he rides in his flaming chariot. Pursued, he looks behind him to ensure his enemies have not tracked him, and he thinks that he has evaded them again. The horses, stallions with orichalcum fire instead of manes, sense his change of mood and slow their ferocious gallop.

The Golden Man guides his chariot down into a clearing somewhere in a desert. The burning aura about his chariot and its banners fades, the man himself sighs as his carriage rolls to a stop. He turns his face to the sky—his perfect face—and begins to speak.

"Once, your blood betrayed me. Serve me now, and that betrayal is forgotten." *He lowers his gaze, reaches his hand out, and touches my cheek. My skin tingles at the caress, sunbeams in the dark of my soul. My eyes close.*

"Bring her back to me, Cassandra. Bring her back to me so that I can know her once again." *He lowers his eyes further. The sun catches him, makes his skin glow in its fading light.*

My heart breaks.

"Bring her back to me. I cannot now bear eternity without her."

Chapter Eleven

The Next Day

Daphne stretched, her hands to the sky, before sitting at her favorite spot in front of the library. She tucked herself into the shade cast by the leaves, a breeze causing the patterns of sunlight to shift on the ground and ruffling her blue sundress. Her leggings whispered against each other as she adjusted her position.

It's always so warm here. A quick glance about and she returned her Kindle to her bag and retrieved her Bible. *I'm looking forward to winter. Maybe it'll be a bit cooler then.* She smiled to herself as she paged through the book to Exodus. *Might remind me of home.*

Daphne flipped open her notebook and put her pen on top of the page, labeling it with her name, the date, and the class.

"Okay." She set her mouth and focused on the book. "Commandment One." She flipped too far, landing on the page with the last several of the divine laws.

A buzz from her bag interrupted Daphne's thoughts. She sighed, rolled her eyes, and dug out the phone—her mother's picture smiled at her from the screen.

"Hi, Mom."

"Honey! Haven't heard from you in a while, so we wanted to check in. How're things? Are your classes going okay?"

"Sure, Mom. Things are fine." Daphne's eye fell back onto the open page of the Bible and started drifting up the list of rules.

Thou shalt not covet your neighbor's wife.

"Great! Are you doing okay on money? You haven't been going out and buying big-screen TVs or anything, have you?"

Thou shalt not bear false witness against thy neighbor.

"Of course not. I've got better things to do than spend all day watching T.V., Mom."

"Really? Is it too much to hope that you're being distracted by something...by someone else?"

Thou shalt not steal.

"What are you talking about?"

Thou shalt not commit adultery.

"Just hoping that you might have found a special someone to spend your free time with." She laughed. "Or maybe some of your not-so-free time."

Thou shalt not kill.

Daphne sighed, and her attention drifted from the book back to the conversation. "No, Mom. Nothing like that."

"So, no one at all, then? You know, your father had quite the reputation in college." A moment's pause. "I had my own social life, too."

Daphne's eyes recoiled from the phone, landing on the Bible once more. She turned back a page as she laughed. "Mom, just stop. I don't want to hear that stuff."

"All right, all right." Another moment. "You will let me know, won't you?"

Honor thy father and thy mother. Daphne's lip curled at the irony. "Yes, Mom. I'll let you know."

"Okay. How have you been getting along with your roommate?"

"Hmmm?" *Why the hell am I reading these backwards?* Daphne moved her eyes to the top of the page. "What did you say?"

"I asked how you were getting along with your roommate. Chloe, wasn't it?"

Daphne's eyebrow arched as she jotted down the first Commandment. "I don't have a roommate, Mom. I haven't had one since I got here."

This time the pause was longer. "Honey, you told us about her over dinner before we left. You said that you thought you two would be a good match, that you would enjoy being roommates. Did something happen?"

Daphne's pen moved to the next line. "Mom, I don't know what you're talking about. My room was empty when I got there. I asked the R.A. about it, and she said that they'd fill the spot when someone transferred in." She looked to the next Commandment.

Her pen froze.

Thou shalt have no other gods but me.

"Well, I suppose I could be mistaken." Her mother's reply dripped with doubt as if it had been soaked overnight. "So, anything else going on?"

Daphne did not respond. She did not even hear her mother's voice addressing her.

Her eyes were trapped by that line. *Thou shalt have no other gods but me.*

"Sure, Mom." Her hand moved of its own volition, moved to the Bible itself, directing the pen in circles around that Commandment. "I'll talk to you later. Love you."

Scritch.

"What? Honey, are you..."

Beep.

Daphne left the phone where it lay as she stared at the single line of scripture, now encircled several times over in black ink. Her lips formed the words over and over without sound.

Thou shalt have no other gods but me.

Her hand left the Bible and returned to her paper, but her eyes remained focused, nigh unblinking. In some small part of her mind, she knew that this was wrong, that something was terribly, terribly wrong, but she could not detach, could not break away. Pen scratching, writing, scribbling as her eyes traced the words over and over and...

The sun was setting when Daphne felt the tap on her shoulder. Her focus snapped and she was once again in control of herself. She blinked and teared up, seeking the source of the interruption.

White eyes met her blue.

Chapter Twelve

"You know you sound crazy, right?"

Cassandra and Daphne were seated at a Denny's table about a half-hour walk from the campus. The place was full of families enjoying budget dining, and a large, half-full cup of black coffee stood next to Daphne's arm.

"I do know." Cassandra sipped a glass of water. "Believe me, I do." Another sip. "If I wasn't completely certain of what I have seen, I wouldn't believe me either. Especially after the way I treated you before—but you have to understand, things have changed." She smiled, and her smile was beatific, the smile of the pious man who has finally seen the face of God.

Daphne shook her head. "I'm sorry, Cassandra."

"Cassie, please."

"...Cassie. Thanks for the coffee, but I have better things to do than listen to lunatics." She put her hands on the table and began to stand.

"Wait." Cassandra laid her hand over the other woman's. Her royal blue fingernails were a sharp contrast to her pale skin. "Haven't you felt...weird...lately? Like words have two meanings, or there's something you remember clearly that no one else seems to? How about that paper you were writing on when I walked up?"

Daphne swallowed hard and removed her hands from the tabletop, taking a swallow of coffee. "I was just circling one of the Commandments. It...it was for an assignment."

Cassandra laughed. "Do you normally draw so many circles it wears through the paper? Or, how about the fact that you weren't looking at it while you drew it? In fact, it seemed to me that you could hardly take your eyes off this Bible." Cassandra shook her head as she spoke, flipping the pages of Daphne's book. "It's like you were looking for some sort of hidden message." The pages rustled as she closed the cover and slid the book across the table. "You didn't even hear me come up."

Daphne breathed in, searching for a response. Her shoulders sagged when she didn't find one.

"I don't know. You're right; a lot of things *have* been really weird for me lately." Her face hardened. "But it's *much* more likely that I'm going crazy or having some kind of nervous breakdown than the idea that there's something...supernatural going on."

Cassandra *tsked,* causing Daphne to flush red. "Excuses. You're a *writer,* Daphne. You know the power of words, of stories. Don't listen to *logic.* That's the realm of cold hard facts, of cause and effect. Listen to your heart; listen to the birthplace of fantasy, of magic." If Cassandra's eyes were not stark white, Daphne would have been trapped by their intensity. "Reason holds no place in the domains of gods."

Daphne's mouth opened to protest, to decry her companion's words.

This is a result of the world you've grown up in. Golden hair caught the fading sunlight, its owner's mouth drawn in a remorseful smile. Dust danced in the sunbeams between them, and the sadness in his eyes all but drowned her.

"His eyes are green." Cassandra broke in upon Daphne's sudden reverie. "He has the habit of smiling with the left side of his mouth, especially when he's sad. He speaks like a poet or a scholar from hundreds of years ago." She winked. "Does that sound about right?"

Several seconds passed. Daphne's visage roiled along with her thoughts, transitioning from denial to confusion to near despair.

"But..." Her words were pale shadows of the confident woman she had been moments ago. "If you're right...if he's...what does that mean? Where has he been? If he's been hiding or running, why did he show up here, now?"

Cassandra patted Daphne's trembling hand. "I don't know. I don't even know if he does. It doesn't really matter. He's in danger, and he needs you. He wants me to bring you to him, so he can explain everything." She sighed. "I just hope that it doesn't turn out too badly, in the end."

Daphne's eyes were wet, her heart torn in two by confusion. "Why me? Who is he? Who am I to him?" She shook her head once more. "I don't even know what he wants with me. How do you know –"

"I don't know who he is, or why he wants you so badly." Cassandra paused as the server refilled their glasses, waiting for her to leave. "What I am sure of is that he is nothing like you or I have ever seen before." Her smile was wistful, pretty. "All my life, I've seen things that would happen, but no one has ever believed me. There has never been anything I could do to use my gift to help others, to avert disasters, assist the needy. Never. All because they wouldn't *see*, wouldn't listen to the warnings I had." She took a deep breath. "Finally, that's going to change...unless it's too late."

"What do you mean?"

Cassandra waved a hand, dismissing the question. "You wouldn't believe me if I told you. Better to wait so that, when it happens, you can accept it for yourself."

"Have you been able...able to..." Daphne licked her lips and swallowed another gulp of coffee. "...see the future for your whole life?"

Cassandra smiled at her cup. "Since I can remember. No one believes children anyway, and I don't see most things, so it's not like I could have claimed a great track record, but there were times when I could see someone's death or wedding or children clear as I see you now."

She shook her head, laughing. "The funny thing was, even after it came to pass, no one would remember that I had said it. No matter how many times I may have reminded them, no matter how often I was right, it was like it was the first time I had said it."

"Like a deja-vu dream?" Daphne had shed some of her nervous tics and was leaning forward as Cassandra spoke. "Like when you tell them, 'I've dreamed this! Remember when I told you?' And no one ever does, not ever."

Cassandra stood and beckoned Daphne with her hand. "Exactly, right. The worst part was the first vision I had. Apparently, each seer...is that the right word?...has the same first vision." She shuddered as she took her place in the payment line.

"...What was it?"

A moment of silence made Daphne wonder if the event was so bad that Cassandra had closed herself down and gone dark. "If you don't want to tell me, that's O.K., Cassie. Really."

"No, no." Cassandra dropped her Visa down with the receipt at the register. A single tear dropped down her left cheek. "See, it skips generations. Sometimes two, but it's always the same. The white eyes reappear and the older woman tries to prepare the young one for what's going to happen." A small smile, sad and forlorn, crossed Cassandra's face as she signed the credit card receipt. The cashier took it, but avoided looking at his customer.

"My first vision came when I was six." The night air was warm and moist, and clouds shut out the moon and stars. "I saw my grandmother standing in line at her bank. She was wearing dress-up clothes, like she was going to church, and carrying her black handbag." Her eyes flowed more freely, and her voice changed. "As she walks to the teller, she reaches into her bag for her I.D. and money. A strange sound from behind makes her turn around. The first thing she sees is the barrel of a revolver leveled at her head."

Daphne covered her mouth with one hand. "Oh my God."

Cassandra was relentless, speaking even as the words seemed to tear her apart inside. "The person holding the gun is an old man, about her age, and he is crying. His skin is speckled with liver spots, but he cocks the hammer back. She looks at him, nods, and whispers, 'It's okay. You were born to do this.' Then, then the gun fires, and the pain starts. She can feel the blood pouring down her face as she falls, feel her weak hip crack as she hits the ground. Her eyes close as the world fades to black and the last neurons stop firing."

Cassandra seemed to come back to herself, wiping her face with the back of her hand and grabbing a napkin from the dispenser. Daphne watched, her mind racing. *I...I don't think she's making this up. If she is, she deserves a fucking Oscar.*

"...Did you tell her?"

"Yes." Cassandra nodded, her face still red. "I sat down with her and, as best I could at six years old, told her about what I had seen. She sat there and listened to the whole thing, then smiled, sighed, and kissed my forehead." A moment passed. "She told me that she was sorry, but also relieved that the burden would no longer be hers." The girl shook her head. "Of course, I didn't understand what she meant, and she died less than a week later. Exactly the way I had seen it."

Daphne reached out and captured Cassandra in a hug. "I...that sounds so horrible. I'm so sorry."

Cassandra returned the hug, a gentle laugh ringing. "No one would believe me when I told them about what had happened to Grandma. When the police came back confirming everything I had said, none of them could remember me having said it. None at all."

"Wow." Daphne looked up into the night sky at the glow of city lights reflecting off the bottoms of the clouds. "So...you're supposed to bring me...bring me to him? Where is he?"

Cassandra laughed. "How would I know? He didn't give me GPS coordinates or anything like that." Cassandra guided her companion to a public bench and patted the seat beside her. Daphne sat down, her brow furrowing.

"Umm...then what's with the bench?"

Cassandra gestured toward the horizon, where the sky was beginning to pink up; sunrise was coming.

"Wait a minute." Daphne checked the time on her phone. "It's only just past midnight!" She looked up again; the light was brightening, but none of the other people on the street—those driving, walking, or sitting—so much as looked up toward the glowing heavens.

Daphne stared, stared until tears streaked from her eyes, as the sun crested over the buildings, casting shadows over the Florida causeway.

She blinked.

The sun is moving.

She shook her head, rubbed her eyes. *No, it can't be. I must be hallucinating. I...*

She glanced over at her companion; Cassie's face had tipped up toward the glowing sphere, and she was smiling. The warmth spread across Daphne's body, caressing her, filling her, and she turned back to face its source.

The luminous orb seemed to hover a moment over the buildings, then dipped down and resumed its motion, accelerating.

I was not *expecting this when I woke up this morning.* Daphne pinched her leg. *Yep. Awake.* A random thought made her laugh. *Guess the astronomers are going to have to reconsider a few things, aren't they?*

The celestial body rolled down the thoroughfare, slowing to a stop twenty feet from the pair. As Daphne watched, the glow faded, transitioning from blinding through warm to gentle and soft. As the bright light dimmed down, a form, hazy and indistinct at first, began to emerge from within.

From the golden light, the trot of horse hooves echoed off the pavement. Two golden stallions with fire-red manes marched out of the glow, pulling behind them an open chariot, forged from red steel and solid gold. The sides swept up, bearing inlaid sunbursts, and the wheels were burnished—a brilliant, ruddy golden.

The master of the chariot held the leather reins in one hand while he raised the other in greeting. Gold and silver robes flowed from his shoulders, and his smile put the now-faded radiance of his chariot to shame. His green eyes caught Daphne's blue ones, and the sight of them took her breath away.

All of her memories crashed through the dams erected by the magic of the Lethe. In an instant, the last several days rewrote themselves in her mind—falsely-woven memories split along the seams to reveal the patterns of real happenings. Chloe, the battle, the betrayal—everything was made clear again, as well as this strange person who had invaded her life.

She was still in shock when he pulled up next to her and extended his hand.

"Will you come with me now, Daphne? There is much for us to speak of, my love."

"Why?" Daphne's voice shook with emotion. "How can you expect me to trust you?"

"Accompany me, and I promise that everything will be made clear."

She stared at the outstretched fingers for several moments, eyebrow raised, then her eyes moved back to his face.

"I will not harm you as long as I live, Daphne. You have my word upon the great River Styx."

Daphne placed her hand in his. It was warm, the skin soft but the grip firm. A deep heat spread from his fingers to the core of her body.

The golden stranger pulled her up onto the chariot, the motion smooth and easy. Now aboard,

Daphne could see a golden bow, as beautiful as its owner in its own way, propped against the edge of the vehicle.

"Hold on to the chariot, Daphne." The man reached around her to grab the reins, and his scent enveloped her, a mixture of cayenne and honey, sending shivers through her body as if she had been frozen and his presence was warming her and thawing her limbs for the first time. The metal was also warm to her touch, and the horses ahead nickered as they pawed the ground and tossed their heads.

"Let's go." The golden man gave the reins a gentle shake, and the stallions leapt to attention, thundering down the road. The bumps made the chariot rattle and shake on its wheels, and Daphne's grip tightened until her knuckles were white.

The man glanced over at her, his smile beaming out like a searchlight. "Don't worry." He patted her hand with one of his own. "The ride will shortly become much smoother."

He pulled back on the reins just as the road changed to a "T" intersection. Daphne screamed as her center of gravity shifted; the chariot had begun to angle upwards, driving up the side of a multi-story office building.

Why am I not falling? She stood upright on the chariot, even though her feet were perpendicular to the surface of the Earth. Window after window raced by as the vehicle picked up speed. Daphne could see late-night maintenance personnel milling about inside, but not one looked up as the flaming chariot passed.

The chariot crested the building and the horses adjusted their upward trajectory to a gentler slope. Daphne looked over the edge to see the city below them.

"One thing that I have enjoyed watching these last several millennia is the amazing progress humanity has made in spreading out over the globe." The golden man waved his hand out, encompassing the lights below them.

Oh, God. Daphne watched as the man's gesture drew her to look down once again. *How fast are we going?*

The city had already been left behind, and she could see the coastline approaching. "Before you start waxing nostalgic or philosophical or whatever this is, could you please, *please,* explain what the hell is going on?"

The man's face transitioned from jubilant and carefree to remorseful in less than a second. "My apologies." His gaze, once strong and focused, now bounced around like a pinball in a machine.

Daphne's tension broke. Here she was, flying through the air in a flaming chariot with a man who looked like he stepped out of Classical Greek sculpture...and he was *apologizing*?

"I didn't ask for an apology." She shook her head; her hair blazed out in the speeding wind like the fires of the chariot. "I just wanted an explanation before I decide whether or not I'm going to ask you to drop me off at the next bus station to Crazytown."

The man's eyes widened, and a smile broke across his face like the sun smashing through a rift in the clouds. Daphne couldn't help but answer the genuine relief and pleasure in that smile with her own.

"Yes, Daphne." The stranger took her hand in his once more and gave it a gentle kiss. "Answers you will have, once we have reached a place of safety."

Daphne's heart fluttered and burned at the contact of his warm lips; the feeling pulsed through her entire body, weakening her knees. She closed her eyes, took a breath, reopened them. "Where are we going?"

Sparkles erupted over the water below them as the sun crested the horizon. The golden man flicked the reins, and the stallions strained against his grip.

Daphne's eyes were locked on her companion's arms as the muscles bunched and knotted. "How strong are those horses?"

Without taking his eyes from their course, he gave a soft laugh. "No one else in the world can master them." The smile on his lips and around his eyes faded. "And only once has someone tried."

"Oh." The chariot's course had changed; if the sun were actually a burning disc in the sky instead of a far-off star, they would be heading straight for it. Indeed, it seemed to be brightening, and...

Is it getting larger?

Daphne fumbled; she could not put her thought into words. "Umm...are we...is it...?" She shook her head, tried again. "What are we doing?"

The solar disc had expanded to fill a quarter of the sky. "We are returning to a place that has not played host to a guest in over a thousand years." The wind blew away the crystal droplets forming in the corners of his eyes.

"Once, I could hear the calls of the horns announcing my approach. Once, I would pass my sister as she rode her own chariot into the sky. Once, returning here was a cause of celebration."

A momentary pause gave Daphne a chance to speak. "Are you all right?"

His answering smile was strained. "I will be. I do not return here often, as the good memories have been torn away, and a bleeding hole still weeps in my heart."

Daphne's own heart ached as she looked into the despair, thinly veiled, in his eyes. She turned away from his face, and her eyes happened to skate toward the front of the carriage.

The Sun now stretched from horizon to horizon. No blue remained in the sky, only bright, searing white.

She could no longer look away.

A warm, powerful arm wrapped itself around her waist and held her tight as the horses raced toward the burning, shining surface.

A whisper in her ear.

"I've got you."

Interlude

Cassandra watched as the god took his love into the heavens. The radiance swept upward, shadows lengthening until they once again blended with the ambient darkness of the midnight gloom.

She smiled as she turned away. *I hope it works out for you, Daphne.* She began her walk back to the college campus. *Someone like that, it might be hard to live up to your own expectations of yourself.* A laugh. *He might make you forget them.*

Without warning, the world around Cassandra vanished. Instead of the orange-lit streets and buildings, her eyes raked across a scene from a mad scientist's horror film laboratory.

Across from her position were several dozen tubes of various sizes, from hand-sized to larger than a man. Each was marked with scientific labels, but Cassandra could not make out what was written on them. All were filled with a viscous, green fluid, and a plethora of tiny bubbles were entrapped within.

There was also something else. Cassandra leaned forward, her momentum carrying her to the largest of the tubes. Something dark floated within the tank, but the glass was covered with a layer of moisture. Cassandra hesitated, then wiped the beads off the tube next to the strange dark spot.

A single blue eye stared back.

Cassandra jumped, stifling her own scream with her hand. The strange floating object was part of a human head. The skull was cracked along the right side, and the eye-socket on that side was caved in and the eye was gone. The flesh was still on the bone, although creamy-white was visible through the many lacerations across the cheeks and forehead. The lips were pulled back in a phantom grimace, and strands of black and grey hair floated in the thick fluid.

Cassandra's eyes moved, unbidden, as her hand stayed clamped over her own mouth. Hundreds of tubes lined the walls in every direction. Each tube had some object or another within, floating just beyond the range of clear vision.

Her scream could no longer be contained. The shriek tearing from her chest shattered the vision, shredding it into small fragments of rainbow contrails spinning into nonexistence as the woman fell to her knees, unable to process, unable to move.

Cassandra's breath came in quick gasps and her sweat fell in gunshots against the concrete under her hands. The edges of her vision wavered.

Oh no. Not now. Please not now. I wasn't ready.

A sudden red flare cut off any further thought. Consciousness slid into a gaping abyss that opened in response to the screaming pain appearing in the back of her head. Her chin cracked against the ground as she fell, but she did not feel it.

Chapter Thirteen

"My God." Daphne clutched at the golden edge of the chariot. The horses had slowed their charge and were now trotting through the sky. Below swirled a maelstrom of clouds rotating like a hurricane. Through the white and grey blanket thrust a great mountaintop, a spear point aimed at the heavens. It was larger than any mountain Daphne had imagined, and she felt dwarfed by its magnificence.

The stranger's warm hand had covered hers again after he released her from his arm. Daphne's blue eyes glanced down, and she gasped, pulling away from his warm touch. The golden flesh on that hand was now glowing, shedding a soft, comforting radiance that flowed from his skin, his nails.

Daphne's gaze trailed up the muscular arm into the face of a god. The glow seemed, now, no more strange than his smile, simply a part of the divinity who stood before her. She extended her hand toward his face, fearful but unable to stop herself.

"Are...are you Apollo?"

His smile put the beauty around her to shame. The whiteness of his teeth was dazzling in and of itself, but the genuine emotion behind the expression was what took her breath away.

"I cannot tell you what it means to have you call me by my name." He pressed her hand into his cheek; warm tremors ran down her heart as he turned his head and pressed his lips against her palm.

Despite what her body was telling her, Daphne pulled her hand away. "Hold on a second." The chariot began to descend; on the peak of the mountain, white structures were coming into focus. "For the purposes of discussion, let's assume that, somehow, some way, you might actually be the Greek God of the Sun." She pursed her lips, then smiled. "I mean, I've come up with crazier things while writing."

"Such as a conspiracy that conceals the fact mankind has colonized Mars over and over again?"

"I don't know if that idea counts as...wait a minute." She met Apollo's gaze. "How did you know about that? That one's still just on my hard drive."

"I am more than the God of the Sun, you know." The city below was clear now, with great buildings of white marble laid out amongst gold and silver streets. Massive walls enclosed the city in its entirety, but the gates were broken, hanging by a single hinge. The stallions guided the craft toward that entrance. "I am...I *was* also the patron of the Muses, goddesses of the Arts."

Daphne's eyes brightened. "The Muses? Really? Can I meet them?"

The smile disappeared from Apollo's face and the radiance around him seemed to dim. The chariot touched down outside the ruined gates and the horses slowed to a walk as they passed through. On either side rose edifices and structures that reminded Daphne of pictures she had seen in her history and mythology books—the Parthenon, Greek and Roman forums.

Directly ahead was a massive palace, columns of marble and polished granite stretching over a football field's length into the air. Great statues, more than a dozen in all, stared out toward the rest of the city from between the columns. A thunder cloud stood above the palace, a black and grey cotton lit by flashes of lightning within.

"...Apollo?"

The god shook his head, forcing a smile.

"To answer your last question first." He paused, looking past the landscape around them to something much further away. "You will not be able to meet the muses."

Daphne opened her mouth to speak, but something about Apollo's face made the words falter in her mouth.

"They were beautiful, you know. Embodiments of the creative spirit, never bored, never boring. Beautiful in body and mind, all of them. Their loss has been felt in your world for quite some time." He shook his head and pulled on the reins, bringing the great stallions to a stop before a glorious stable. The doors were stained cedar and the stalls at least twice the size of those for mortal horses. Apollo dismounted and raised a hand to help Daphne off the chariot.

"For so long, we thought we would always be the favored gods of the West." He unhitched the horses and gave them a gentle pat; heads high, they moved into their stalls and began munching from their enormous feed bags. Apollo smiled as he watched, but his voice was solemn. "The Roman Empire rose, but their gods were weak, barely formed. We replaced them, taking their names and adapting to the Roman ideal, but otherwise unchanged. Our power waxed and our primacy remained, even as other faiths were born."

Apollo brought Daphne around the corner of the building adjacent to the stable. "What happened?"

A short laugh, bitter, harsh. "Constantine."

Daphne's brow wrinkled. "The Roman Emperor?"

"Yes. He declared Christianity to be the official religion of Rome." Apollo pushed open the golden double-doors; inside, the sun shone into an open hall, filled with gleaming statues, cascading fountains, and ever-full cornucopia with grapes and pomegranates spilling over. Warm breezes stirred hair and tickled noses. Apollo closed his eyes as he took a deep breath, and Daphne was again struck by him.

My God. The thought recurred as her eyes traced the line of his jaw, the curve of his cheek. *He really is –*

"Is there something on my face, Daphne?

Shit! Her cheeks flared to match her hair as her brain fumbled for an answer. "I...I was just waiting for you to finish your story."

"Ah." He nodded, but a trace of the smile remained.

"Did Christianity somehow...remove your power? Undercut the people who believed in you, weaken you?"

Apollo motioned for Daphne to sit at a small table, one which had a small fountain burbling a purple liquid and a cornucopia sprouting fruits. He followed after her. "Are you hungry?"

Daphne shook her head, but the sudden grumbling in her stomach betrayed her. She grabbed a bunch of red grapes and began popping them into their mouth, only slowing when she saw the Sun God watching her, suppressing a laugh.

"Will you stop?" Daphne forced her mouthful of grapes down and chased it with a goblet of water so she could speak. "I don't know when the last time you were around humans was, but we generally don't like getting stared at." She picked up another grape. "Especially while we eat."

"I have spent a great deal of time amongst mortals, actually." Apollo reached into the purple fountain and withdrew a glittering crystal cup. "Both recently and when I was worshiped across the Peninsula and beyond. However." The god leaned forward and captured her eyes with his own, green holding blue. "It is the first time that I have gotten to watch *you* eat, and I am greatly enjoying it."

"Oh." Daphne chewed and put her cup back to her mouth to hide the ever-present blush. *Am I ever going to be able to just talk without making a fool out of myself?*

Apollo sipped his drink. "To answer your question, I am now worshipped by several million people across the Earth. Not as many as there once were, certainly –"

"Wait." Daphne put her glass down. "Millions still worship you? Like, really?"

"I hear their prayers. I smell their offerings. I grant them aid when I can, although that is not as often as I would like." He shrugged and took another sip. "I have not noticed my strength weakening. My will to use it, perhaps, but my power remains."

"Then how did Christianity tie into it?"

A short, snorting laugh. "I have never met the Christian God, personally, but I have met many of His followers. In the beginning, they were a repressed people, forced to conceal their faith for fear of execution or banishment. With Constantine's declaration, they were liberated."

Apollo put his goblet back onto the table; the liquid within rocked back and forth. "Imagine, Daphne, that you were a prisoner. You were forced to lie, to hide that which was most precious to you, most important to your sense of self. Then, suddenly, the shackles are cast off you and you are free. What would you do?"

Daphne considered, twirling her cup in her hands and staring into it. "I think I would...I think I would celebrate. Rejoice in my freedom. I don't know."

She shook her head, then raised it, her eyes searching Apollo's face.

He was grinning. "Then you are a better woman than most. Most would take revenge on those who had oppressed them."

Daphne hesitated. "Is...is that what happened?"

Apollo breathed out and closed his eyes. The silence stretched out, but Daphne waited.

"Yes." Apollo nodded his head. "That is what happened."

A single tear ran from his closed eyelids. Daphne's hand reached out for his...but she pulled it back before touching him.

"They came at us. Armed with chants and relics of their faith, a small group of believers stormed Olympus and caught the gods by surprise. My father never saw them coming."

Daphne leaned in, the story unfolding in her mind, Apollo's words laying the scene out before her. "How did they get in?"

"I never knew." The Sun God spoke in a flat monotone, a survivor of a tragedy he still couldn't cope with. "There were twenty of them, in capes of white and red, bearing the sign of the Cross. They broke through the gates with their spells and began their slaughter."

Daphne's writer-brain was filtering the words into pictures: soldiers screaming admonitions and prayers descended upon hapless spirit attendants, cutting them to pieces.

"My half-brother Ares was the first to fall. He stood before the invaders with his blade dripping blood, and he bellowed his challenge...but it was cut short by the blessed dagger that appeared in his throat."

Daphne's hand covered her mouth. "Oh my God."

"We aren't easy to kill, you see. Only power equal to our own can truly do us harm, so no one was expecting Ares to be injured, let alone slain. Hephaestus was next; he was too slow to run away. His Cyclopes fought to the last to cover his retreat, but a spear took him as he fled. Every one that was there, all present for the feasting and the revelry, died that day. There was so much death that I couldn't keep track of it all—after the death of my father everything faded away—but I saw the aftermath clearly enough." Apollo's face hardened and he slammed a fist onto the table, causing Daphne to start. "The bastards waited in the homes of my family, waited for the rest of them to return, and ambushed them. Eris was destroyed so thoroughly that nothing was left of her, taken by more than a dozen Crusaders. Nike tried to rally the rest, but...in the end, none survived, save a few minor nymphs and nature spirits."

Daphne hesitated to ask the question burning on her tongue. "...How did you escape?" Her voice was a whisper, afraid of his response but full of her need to know. "Why didn't they get you?"

The God's green eyes closed. "The attack came during the day. I never came back."

"Why not?"

He turned to her and looked her in the face. "Because I knew it was happening."

The silence echoed through the chamber.

"I have always been an Oracle." Apollo took another drink. "Able to see the future, important events."

"So you know everything before it happens?"

Apollo shook his head. "I see portents. Omens. Glimpses of things to come. They must be interpreted, but..." He tapped himself on the forehead. "I have many, many years' experience of doing so. I am rarely wrong."

"I guess not. But you don't get omens...about everything?"

"Not at all. I didn't know I would be encountering you, for instance." He smiled as Daphne fidgeted in her seat, flushing once more. "It was a pleasant surprise."

Daphne nodded, trying her best to focus on his words and not on the effect he was having on her.

"So, yes, I knew, and I tried to warn my family, but they refused to believe me. Even wise Athena, who said that what I had seen was impossible. 'This God is not real,' they said. 'How can soldiers of a nonexistent God overpower us? We have not seen him, have not heard him.'"

"Well, I guess that makes sense, in a way. I mean, you guys were used to knowing what you were dealing with, right?"

"It was a specious argument!" Apollo roared, and Daphne was thrown back in her chair as the shockwave splintered glass, scattered wine and water, and threw a shiver into the air. "They were fools. They had seen the gods of other peoples, even as Rome had spread and conquered them, but those people's faiths still held power. I have seen holy men and women of every faith perform miracles at the behest of their gods. Who gives them this power, if their gods are not real? Who, I asked them, resurrected this Christ if his God was not real?"

Apollo's voice and the vibrations it left in the air ceased; Daphne's chest rose and fell in deep, rapid breaths, and she held the arms of her chair. The sungod fell back into his own seat, spent.

"When I came back, they were all gone. The warriors had taken the bodies of my family away to somewhere I still have not found. Even Hades was lost. I imagine the deaths of so many immortals drew his attention and curiosity and, being a god himself, he was not afraid to investigate." Apollo began to weep, his chest hitching in deep, sobbing cries and rivulets of orichalcum running down his face, coursing off his chin and jaw.

Daphne watched as he cried openly, his radiance flickering and waning as he gave voice to his sorrow. She reached a hand toward him and laid it on his shoulder.

"I'm sorry." She whispered it again as she pulled herself to him and laid his head on her shoulder. His scent tickled her nose and warmed her body, and she was very aware of the contours of his arms and chest as they pressed against her.

Even so, she held him as he wept, pouring out the tears held back over centuries, letting them flow freely down his immortal countenance. She closed her eyes as his sobs began to slow, hoping that her presence was calming to him, soothing.

She stiffened as she felt Apollo's fingers touch her shoulder. They traced gentle lines down the length of her arm, around the bend of her elbow, and to her hand before beginning again. Each caress was hot fire on her skin, melting gold into her flesh and blood. A low moan escaped her lips, and she shuddered.

"What are –" Daphne's words were cut off by Apollo's lips on hers. Warmth flowed from the kiss into her mouth, leaving her stunned and breathless when he pulled away smiling.

"I've been wanting to do that for a very long time."

Daphne blinked. Apollo's face fell, the smile disappearing like mist. "Are you all –"

She reached behind his head, tangling her fingers in his hair and pulling him back toward her. Lips crushed onto lips, heat passing back and forth in the embrace. When they broke apart again, Daphne traced the line of his mouth with her fingertip.

"Does that answer your question?"

She moved back in, pressing her body against his. She could feel the warmth that the god's body radiated, and she wanted all of it. Her arms wrapped around Apollo as her mouth kissed him over and over again, on his lips, his neck, his face.

"Oh, God!" She gasped as Apollo's hands moved, running up her leggings and grasping her hips, lifting her on top of him. She could feel the hard length of him beneath her, and electricity shot up her body and made her gasp.

Daphne threw herself back into the kisses, hands running over every inch of Apollo she could reach. Her hands slipped under the opening of his robe, feeling the hair and musculature of his chest on her own skin for the first time. She savored the feel of his sex against hers, and pressed down into him.

"It's...it's just...I..." Lust consumed the young woman, causing her thoughts to blur into a red haze of sensation. She bent her neck, lips now on Apollo's chest, hands searching for a seam, a gap, something. His hands came up to grasp hers, and Daphne stopped the rain of kisses.

Then his robe vanished, and his golden body lay exposed to her hungry eyes.

"Oh." Daphne trailed her fingers down his carved musculature, down the line dividing his chest, tracing the contours of his abdominals. Apollo reached out again, grasping the folds of Daphne's sundress and lifting.

She raised her arms to allow the garment to pass over her head, the fabric blocking her view for a moment. The Olympian air was cool on her now exposed skin, and her nipples throbbed with need. Both hands locked behind her lover's head and pulled him to her breast, moaning again as he took her into his mouth.

It's never felt anything like this before. Daphne rolled her hips, the thin fabric she still wore the only barrier between herself and consummation. Every action, every touch sent those sparks of burning electricity to her brain, short-circuiting any consideration except the fulfillment of desire. She brought one of his hands to her lips and kissed it, small suckles on the palm and fingers. The other slid down her hip, lingering on the line between the pale panties and the pale skin before slipping underneath. She buried her face in his neck as his fingers entered her –one, two, three—and she bit down as they began their smooth, slow strokes.

"Oh...oh, God...yes..." Daphne's hips stopped their roll and began to thrust in concert with Apollo's movements. "So good...no more, please."

Apollo stopped and backed up enough to look into her face. The left side of his mouth curled in a smile as Daphne stood up to remove her leggings and panties. She enjoyed the attention as the god's green eyes watched her every movement, roving over her flesh as his hands had been just moments ago.

Naked now, Daphne felt her passion surge, stronger than it had been. "I...I need you, Apollo. God, it's like I've been needing you since I saw you, almost."

Apollo stood as well, coming over and embracing her once more. "I have wanted you longer than you can possibly imagine, my love." In a smooth motion, he grasped Daphne's thighs and lifted her up. Even caught in the moment, she still had time to marvel at his strength.

She wrapped her legs around his waist, feeling him press against her. Their eyes locked.

Daphne eased herself down on Apollo, the sensation of his hardness filling her overwhelming her senses. She shuddered as pleasure rippled through her body, locking her muscles for several seconds before she was able to move again. Apollo pressed her against the nearest wall, and, after Daphne's momentary paralysis passed, began to thrust into her.

Daphne's body was awash in sensation, each feeling a different hue in the rainbow of pleasure she was becoming. She wrapped her arms around Apollo's neck, moving her hips, kissing the salt from his skin, gasping each time their bodies collided. Her senses coalesced into a single tactile experience, her brain drowning in animal lust as the pair grunted, moaned, and poured their passion into each other.

Daphne had no sense of time passage, of fatigue, of anything except the continuous pulsing heat of her flesh against the god's, but she felt a surge of triumph when Apollo's thrusting became more urgent and his muscles tensed under her fingers and legs.

"Yes!" Daphne matched him thrust for thrust, feeling her own release building, promising to dwarf all the others. She kissed Apollo again, her mouth seeking to draw his very essence from him as he came, pouring that essence into her. They were locked together, woman and divinity, human and god both helpless in the face of passion.

~~~

Daphne awoke in a huge four-poster bed, silken sheets laying upon her skin like a breeze. The sunlight filtered in through the vast openings in the ceiling, tickling Daphne's face with warmth. She opened her eyes, only to be met by Apollo's smiling green ones.

"Hello." Apollo kissed her forehead, then propped himself on his elbow as he looked down at her. "Nice to see you."

The smell of their lovemaking still clung to them, and, breathing it in, Daphne's mind teased her with the memory for a moment before she was
~~~

able to respond. Her skin filled with blood and one hand clutched at the sheets over her chest.

"...Hi." An echo of the previous night's need washed over her. "Is it...is it morning?"

"That depends on where you are." Apollo smiled. "But, yes, in Florida it is morning right now. You have been asleep for a while."

Daphne returned the smile. "I...Can we talk about what happened?"

"If you'd like." Apollo tossed the sheets off and put his feet on the ground. Sunbeams merged with his golden skin before his robes reappeared, shimmering in the morning light. A thin circlet materialized in his hair, delicate leaves intertwined with the strands. "Are you hungry?"

Daphne opened her mouth to protest, but the sudden grumbling of her stomach gave her away. She gave a crooked smile. "...I guess so." She glanced around the room, which seemed to be blurry, clouded by the sunlight.

"Your glasses are on that pedestal, with your clothes."

"Oh." *Goddamn glasses.* She reached out and grasped the wire frames, slipping them onto her face. The room snapped back into focus. Her dress and other garments were folded in a neat pile.

"Do you mind?"

Apollo's smile turned wicked. "No, not at all. Go right ahead."

Daphne turned an even deeper shade of red. "Fine, then." She stood up, letting the sheet fall from her as she did so, pretending she didn't notice Apollo's eyes raking her body while she dressed. When the sundress passed over her head and she was finished adjusting it, she turned to look her companion full in the face.

Apollo waved his hand, the sleeve of his robe moving to reveal a small table bursting with delicacies. Grapes poured from a crystal bowl beside plates of muffins and ham. The aroma wafted into the air, tickling Daphne's nose and triggering another stomach growl.

Daphne pulled out the chair and sat down. Apollo joined her, pouring a deep red juice from a delicate decanter. "I hope you enjoy your meal. It has been a long time since I entertained a guest here."

Daphne fought to keep her fingers under control; the sight and smell of food had gone straight to her stomach, and all she wanted was to grab something in each hand and shovel it down her throat. Instead, she broke off a small piece of blueberry muffin and chewed, washing it down with a drink of the juice.

Pomegranate. She sighed, closing her eyes. *Of course it'd be pomegranate.*

When she opened them, Apollo was watching her, his hand moving to caress her cheek.

"Why?" Daphne grabbed hold of Apollo's hand, ignoring the tremor of memory from the touch of his skin. "I don't understand. Why me? You've been...I don't know...*pursuing* me since we met, it seems like."

Apollo blinked, his smile faltering. "Have I offended you?"

"No!" *Damn. That was loud.* "...No. It's just that I don't get it. You could have any girl. Hell, you could probably have any guy, too. Why me? Why are you interested in me?"

"Ah." Apollo turned his hand, his fingers stroking the back of Daphne's as he spoke. "Once, long ago, my cousin Eros was shooting in the woods. When I saw him, I teased the child for using a man's weapon. I was proud of my skill with the bow, you see, and I did not think he was worthy of the weapon I myself wielded." A thin smile stretched his lips. "He disagreed."

Dim memories of stories read tickled Daphne's mind. "What did he do? Challenge you to a shooting contest or something?"

"Worse. He loosed a golden-tipped arrow into my heart as a wood nymph ran by. Her red hair streamed in the sunlight, and her feet were bare, and the leaves grew beneath them. In that instant, I loved her with all my being." He shook his head. "I had never experienced the direct impact of his power before. It truly laid me low."

Daphne let out a gasp as faint recollections of stories were replaced by replays of dreams. Recent ones.

"But she didn't love you." Daphne's chest began to burn, and she rubbed the space over that spot as she spoke. "Eros loosed another arrow at the nymph, and she fled you, ran from you, and you pursued her."

Apollo winced. "I did."

There was wonder in Daphne's voice. "Her father heard her cries and turned her into a tree."

"A laurel tree." He fingered the golden crown about his head. "Something I took as my symbol, to remind me always."

Daphne took her hand from the golden god's. Her stomach churned, and her mouth was dry. "So...the reason you're attracted to me...the reason we slept together...is because of magic? Because you were enchanted? *Compelled?*"

"I-"

Daphne shook her head and stood up, backing away. Tears threatened. "You...you son of a bitch."

"Daphne, you *are* that nymph. Somehow, you have been reborn."

"And that matters to me why?" She stepped forward and jabbed her finger into the god's chest, her voice rising. "Maybe a whole lot of weird shit has happened, but I'm not prepared to believe that I'm some two-thousand year old creature reincarnated."

Her lower lip quivered and she turned her head away from him. "You told me you loved me, looked into my eyes while you fucked me, but the whole time it was that nymph you thought you were with."

She turned back and slapped Apollo across the face. His eyes widened, but he made no move to stop her.

"You're the God of the Sun. It's not like I was expecting to be your one and only, the best you'd ever had." Her chest was hitching, but anger pushed her words from her closing throat. "But I thought you were at least interested in *me!* Not...not some shadow, some goddamn memory." She crossed her arms, retreating against a wall. "No. Either take me home or leave me alone and I'll figure it out myself. I'm not going to be with someone who thinks of another woman every time he kisses me. No."

Apollo's face was thunderstruck. His jaw stood agape for several seconds. Daphne stared, waiting, refusing to break the silence first.

"You misunderstand." Apollo took a step closer, then spread his hands in front of him in a "peace" gesture. "Magic made me love the nymph, but I never knew her. It was an all-consuming desire that Eros engendered within me."

Daphne closed her eyes.

"I pined for her for over a hundred years before I was able to let go of that need. I visited the tree every night, and only Father's command would tear me away."

She couldn't hold her tongue. "So? What does that have to—"

"Please." He licked his lips. "I never forgot, although I went on. When I saw you, when we ran into each other at your school, I was shocked. In an instant, I was swept away, taken back to the first moment I saw y...saw the nymph. The old desire came forward, and I kissed you."

Then I kicked you in your goddamn head. Despite her anger and hurt, Daphne had to suppress a laugh. *Served you right.*

"So I spoke to Cassandra. As a Seeress, she was receptive to my message. She brought you to me, and I was able to truly meet you." He tipped his head down, keeping his eyes on her. "I marveled in your voice, your gestures. The pain you felt as I told you my story, how you almost cried with me. I drowned in your eyes as you asked, questioned, and your laughter carried my heart away with it."

Daphne folded in on herself, trying to shut out the emotion in Apollo's voice.

He took another step. "It was magic that made me love the nymph you once were, yes." Step. "It was the memory that made me pursue you." Step. "But it was *you* I was with last night, and no other."

He stopped an arm's length away. She said nothing.

"I ask only one thing. Stay for an hour. I will leave you, and you can think on your decision. If you choose to depart, I will not argue, and, if you wish it, I will never bother you again."

You should go. He can't treat you this way. The thoughts were almost another voice speaking to her. *How dare he?*

"Fine." Daphne didn't look at him. "One hour."

A breeze blew through the room, ruffling the bedcurtains. She glanced up.

Apollo was gone.

<center>~~~</center>

Daphne grabbed a pillow from the bed and threw it at the place he had been standing. The tears she had fought so hard to hold back in his presence surged, and she made no attempt to stem the flow.

Well, what the hell were you expecting, Daphne? She sat on the marble floor, the stone warm beneath her. *Happily ever after? Is that the way it works?*

"Of course not." She exhaled a quavering breath. "But I thought—"

He's a God. You've read the stories. How many sons did he have? How many mortals did he lay with? Fire burned within her mind, almost foreign. *How many goddesses?*

The realization crushed the small spark of hope that Daphne still held. "Yeah. Goddesses. The Muses."

Forever beautiful. Forever creative.

She nodded to herself; her eyes were red, but the tears had stopped. "I can't live like that, always worrying that he was only with me because of some magic spell."

You should go. Leave him.

Daphne thought, biting her lip, then shook her head. "No. There's too much here." She set her jaw and stood. "If he's telling the truth, I'm the first person to see this in thousands of years. It's fucking *Olympus.*"

You can't win him.

"I don't need to." She straightened her clothes, smoothed her hair with her hands. "What's done is done. I'm not some love-struck schoolgirl, following after him and wishing he would notice the real me just because we slept together. He tells a good story and there's a lot here I want to learn."

...And then?

"Then we're done. 'Thanks for the tour, see you later.'" She took a deep breath. "Apollo? I'm ready to talk."

With as little fanfare as his departure, the Sun God reappeared. His face was tight, pinched. His lips were drawn, and his eyes skittered over her like a frightened mouse.

"...Have you made a decision?"

"I have." *Let him suffer for a few seconds.*

"And?"

"I will stay. For now." She crossed her arms. "But when I say it's time to go, it's time to go. Agreed?"

The relief that washed over his face almost broke Daphne's cold exterior.

Almost.

"I'm glad that you understood." He smiled and stepped toward her. "I had hoped that—"

Daphne shook her head, then raised a finger. "No. This isn't about that. There's too much here and I'm not going to let...a misunderstanding...ruin my chance to see this." Another pause, and Daphne sat down at the table, picking up a strawberry. "So what now?"

Apollo sat across from her. "Next, I show you around Olympus."

Interlude

Cassandra blinked her eyes as consciousness faded in. Sensations were first—metal around her wrists and ankles, something heavy in her arm at her elbow—then sounds. She could hear scribbling, footsteps. The telltale whine of electronics.

She was lying down.

A male voice pierced the fog. "She's waking up, Commander." There was a pause, more footsteps. "Her vitals are still good."

The world began to blur into moving shapes, darks against lights, blues and whites. "Should I sedate her again?"

"Not just yet." This voice was female, and familiar.

Where have I heard her before?

"Cassandra?" A blonde blur stepped to the side of the groggy girl. Cassandra tried to focus her swimming vision on the speaker. "Can you hear me?"

"Where am I?' Cassandra's eyes lolled in her head, unresponsive to her mental commands. "What's going on?"

"Good to see you awake." Out of the hazy, indistinct surroundings emerged a woman in a uniform, white with a red cross emblazoned on the front.

"...Chloe?"

Chloe nodded. "Yes, Cassandra. How have you been? Still creeping people out with those prophecies that no one believes? Must be terrible, to be separated from everyone like that."

Cassandra felt like her brain had left a few cars back at the station. "Wh...what...what's..."

"What's going on? It's simple." Chloe leaned in, her smile sharp enough to wound. "I'm looking for someone. You know where he went. You're going to tell me."

Sudden realization struck, penetrating the drug and trauma-induced fog. "You...you're looking for the golden man, aren't you?"

"Ah, the cloud lifts!" Chloe laughed as she walked around to the head of the hospital-style bed, out of Cassandra's vision.

"Why would I tell you where he is? Even if I did know, I wouldn't."

Chloe ran one hand over the intravenous line which led into the other woman's arm. "Several reasons, I imagine. First off, you don't want to die."

A chill ran down Cassandra's spine, but she did not respond.

"That's not the only reason, though." A syringe appeared in Cassandra's peripheral vision. "It's amazing how much more effective conventional truth agents are when you add a little bit of magic to them. Humans truly are inventive creatures, aren't they?" Chloe flicked the needle and squeezed out a tiny bit of the fluid. "A tiny touch of Aphrodite's sweat makes people's tongues just fly out of control, *begging* to tell us what they know." She winked. "It's the pheromones."

A swift motion and the needle was in the IV junction, its contents beginning their voyage through Cassandra's veins.

"But third, and most importantly, this...friend of ours finally made a mistake. He has defeated us for centuries because he could see what we were going to do next."

Chloe's eyes bored into Cassandra's.

"We finally have something to even the playing field."

Chapter Fourteen

"Okay, I have to admit, *this* is pretty awesome."

Daphne moved her eyes over the view before her—it seemed she could see the entire world, as if she were an eagle flying above it. Thousands of miles stretched out in all directions.

"This was my father's palace." Apollo stood a respectful distance away, near the opening to the balcony. "He would stand here often, gazing upon his dominion and basking in the prayers of our worshipers."

"Is it...is it true what the stories say about him?" Daphne did not turn; the sensation of *seeing* had captured her. Her awareness flew over mountains and oceans, scaled ice-swept peaks and passed over vast, barren deserts.

"That he was...lecherous? Lush? That he could not help himself when presented with a beautiful woman?"

Like you? She stifled the knee-jerk response; the tone of Apollo's words drew Daphne's sympathy. "I'm sorry, Apollo. I keep asking these questions, but it's easy to forget that they were your family." He nodded. "We can talk about something else, if you want."

Apollo waved off her comment. "No, please. It has been a very long time since I was able to share stories with another." His smile returned. "It is nice."

No, don't smile back.

The corners of her mouth lifted. *Goddamn it.* "So..."

"Yes, for the most part. He was. Despite all the times it came back to haunt him, it was as if he labored under some sort of compulsion." Apollo laughed and rapped on his breastbone with his fingertips. "Many of his children matured into great heroes, great warriors, or wise counselors. Many others...did not." Apollo spread out his arms as if to embrace something larger than himself. "I dare say that many descendants of Greece and Rome are my own distant brethren, even today. His blood may even run in your family, you know."

"I hope not." Daphne tipped her head. *It's like he was born to tell stories.* She turned away again, her teeth clenching. *Stop it.*

"Did you ever get jealous?"

He turned his head back to her, brow furrowed.

"I mean, of all his children."

"Ah." He chuckled, happy memories playing on his face. "From time to time, I suppose. Not often. There were a few times I was tempted to do something about Heracles, but after mother Hera began her campaign against him, I decided that he had enough troubles ahead."

This made Daphne laugh.

"Hey." She pointed up at the sky. "How long have we been here? The sun hasn't moved, but it seems like we've been walking and talking for hours."

"Days, more like." Apollo looked off into the distance. "Three so far. You see, on Olympus, those who belong here do not hunger or thirst unless they choose to, do not tire unless they desire slumber. The day lasts until I bid it to pass into the veil of night, and night until my sister relinquishes it to me."

"But...what happens now? I mean –"

"I do not know." Apollo touched his forehead with his fingertips, then held them toward the solar disc. "It has not been night here in hundreds of years."

"...Since then?"

"Yes."

A comfortable silence settled over the pair. Daphne returned to the edge of the balcony, overlooking the world.

"Why?" She spoke into the wind, but she knew Apollo could hear, knew he would understand the question. "Why would they do this?"

Apollo stepped up beside her. "They say it is the will of their God, that there should be no other gods at all." His hands grasped the railing.

"Do you think they're right? Is it the will of God?"

Apollo snorted a laugh. "If it is, then He's done a poor job of it. After all, it's been centuries, but I still live. No matter what they've tried, they have not been able to change that."

"Why don't you just stay here?" Daphne gestured to the beauty surrounding them, the marble gleaming and the blue expanse of sky. "Wouldn't it be safer?"

Another laugh. "I'm safe enough, my l...Daphne." He rubbed the back of his neck. "I know when they plan anything—an attack on the last living god is important enough to the Weaving that it attracts my attention every time."

Daphne returned his smile; it was almost impossible not to. "Not full of yourself or anything, are you?"

"Well, I *am* unique." Apollo tipped Daphne a wink. "But it's more than that. Gods are tangled in the threads of fate and destiny. Everything we do changes history. It's easy for an oracle to see the actions of a god...or the death of one."

Despite the warmth, Daphne shivered under the impact of that phrase. She rubbed her arms to banish the chill.

"More important, though, is that I would not desire to remain here for long." His amused attitude faded, his smile vanishing like the sun hiding behind a sky of grey clouds. "My family was murdered here, and I can still see the bloodstains on the walls, the bodies of the servants, all of it."

"Oh." Daphne winced. *Open mouth, insert foot. Way to go, Daph.* "Yeah. That...that makes sense."

"Fortunately, there is no danger to me at the moment." Apollo stood and held his hand out to Daphne as he continued. "And there are prayers to attend to as well, if I can manage. Do you wish to wait for me here? Or should I drop you off somewhere on Earth?"

Daphne could feel the real question Apollo was asking beneath the one he had given voice to. She chewed on her lip, then grabbed one of the ever-present chalices of dark red liquid to buy herself some time.

"What *is* this?" She pulled the cup back from her lips and blinked in amazement. "It tastes different every time I have some."

Apollo grinned. "That is nectar. It is the only drink that a god in his true form can be nourished by. Although we do not need it, as I explained, it can replenish energy or soothe the spirit."

"Wait. Nectar?" Daphne reappraised the drink. "Isn't that for gods only?"

"Customarily. We do, however, have an excess of supply right now."

"Ah."

"There is also the fact..." Apollo trailed off, licked his lips as he watched Daphne take another drink, then shook his head. "Never mind."

Daphne opened her mouth to protest, then shook her head and closed it. *I've pressed him enough; he's given enough secrets. Probably best that he keeps one.*

"I've never been to a worship ceremony for a pagan god." She nodded. "I don't think I should miss that."

Apollo broke into a massive smile; he seemed unable to contain his joy. "I have not had a companion on my journeys for some time." He offered her his arm to take. "Shall we?"

Daphne arched her eyebrow. "Try any of that shit and you can call the whole thing off."

Apollo's face fell, and he lowered his arm. "Of course. My apologies."

Chapter Fifteen

"They really can't see us?"

The small space was lit by the noon sunlight, white and grey stone reflecting it in all directions. Seven white-robed men and women circled an altar in the center of the space, stopping to intone ritual chants, continuing their circumlocution.

"No." Apollo walked forward, stopping a few feet outside the sacred circle. "My power has shrouded us so that we might watch, observe their worship. It would take the eyes of a Seer to find us." He shook his head. "Once, ceremonies like these— not that these are exactly as they were—stretched across the entirety of the Roman Empire, from east to west."

"...Do you miss it?" Daphne came up next to him, watching as the ceremony progressed. The two leaders, one male and one female, lowered their hoods and stepped to the center of the circle, embracing. "Miss being the center of the universe?"

Apollo's head snapped around, eyes narrowed, but when he saw Daphne's crooked smile, he relaxed. "Sometimes. Mostly, it is simply pleasant to not be responsible for so many, to have civilization's well-being in my hands." He swept his arm toward the gathering. "Now, when it pleases me, I visit these groups and, if I choose, grant their prayers." A small chuckle.

I bet you do. "Why the laugh?"

"Just remembering a discussion I once had with Dionysus. He claimed that we would be worshiped as fervently if we never appeared, that all that was necessary was to tell the faithful that our inaction was, in fact, action. I disagreed."

He sighed. "I was wrong."

Daphne wrinkled her brow, looked back toward the congregation as they broke the service and began mingling with one another. "What do you mean?"

"If I grant their prayers, they may or may not attribute it to my intervention." He raised a finger. "But, if I do not, they may still attribute that to my judgment, claiming that I had decided not to do so, for my own reasons, unknown to them."

"I see. There are those who worship...what should I call him?"

Apollo's eyebrows rose. "Who?"

Daphne fluttered her hands as she stammered. "I...fine. The Christian...or Jewish...or –"

"Ah." Apollo reached out a hand and put it on Daphne's shoulder, and she felt his warmth melting the tension away before he removed it. "Do not be afraid of offending me. The name I prefer is that given to him by some of his followers. I call him Jehovah—easily recognized by most when I speak of him, not so strange that it draws attention."

Daphne swallowed. "Okay...so, some worshipers of Jehovah, claim that same thing, that when he doesn't grant their prayers, it is a test of faith and that it should make them believe all the more."

"I have never seen Jehovah grant a prayer." Apollo's voice had settled into a near-monotone. "I have never seen him intervene, nor any of his agents, the angels, the demons. I have felt his power from afar, seen it in my visions, watched as it tore my family to pieces, but never him, never the being himself." He shrugged, but his face was sad. "I imagine it must be hard for his followers, to have a god that seems to care so little about them."

"I think that they –"

"Wait, Daphne." Apollo held his hand up, cutting off her speech. "This is important."

Daphne clipped her teeth together.

"I answer prayers because I must. It is the same as breathing, for me. It was always this way." He shrugged. "All the gods that I have known, all those that were cast down, we answer prayers. Not all of them, but we listen, we consider, we care. Why does Jehovah not do this? Why does he not exert his power, bring order, bring comfort to his people? Why does he not bring rain to those under drought, or lift the illnesses of the faithful?"

Daphne waited until Apollo looked her way, eyes questioning.

"I...I don't know." She pursed her lips, licked them, went on. "Maybe Jehovah doesn't care at all, or maybe he's just some sort of impersonal force, like a defining characteristic of the universe. You said that the ones that kill...that attacked your home were wielding his power, but what does that mean? Maybe they're just accessing some kind of universal law." She shrugged. "I don't know."

"A sad universe indeed, if the true Creator of it all cares so little for his creation." Apollo nodded, looked up toward the sky, then laughed. "I don't suppose that it matters much, anyway, does it?" He opened his arms again, embracing the gathering before him. His voice began to crack. "If I can bring something to these people, if they have chosen me and my family over him, then that means something, doesn't it?"

"I suppose it does." She caught herself before she put a hand on his shoulder. "Why don't we go get something to eat?"

Apollo laughed. "Are you hungry already?"

"No." Daphne wrinkled her nose. "I think I just need a little bit of normality right now. I've almost forgotten what normal people are like."

"Very well. I know this Greek restaurant…"

~~~

Daphne took another bite of her gyro sandwich, rolling her eyes and moaning in pleasure as the flavor flooded her mouth. Apollo chuckled and sat back in his chair, watching her.

"This is amazing." The words were obscured by the sandwich still in her mouth. "How did you find this place?"

"Gregorio came over to the United States about forty years ago." Apollo indicated a portly old fellow who was bustling from table to table, smiling as he conversed with his customers and commanded his staff. "His parents taught him how to cook, and he paired up with a few other immigrants to build this restaurant." The god smiled. "It's become a national chain, and he plans to expand it into other countries as well."

"Well, he definitely deserves it." Daphne dragged her finger along some of the cucumber sauce on her plate, then brought it to her lips. "I guess quality does count for something in this
~~~

world. I wouldn't have thought so, with McDonald's and Wal-Mart and all that crap."

"Do you remember how I said that the world had suffered because of the loss of the Muses?" The god raised an eyebrow and smirked as he lifted his hand. Gregorio waved back, bustling over to their table. "Good morning, good morning, sir! I hope that you are enjoying your meal today!"

"Always, Gregorio. How's business going?"

"Fantastic, sir, fantastic! I expect you will be pleased by your portion, yes?" Gregorio knelt down and gave the sun god a hug; Daphne's eyes widened. "I still can never thank you for helping me find the money for this, my restaurant. You have made my prayers come true."

Apollo laughed. "That's what I do, old friend. Can we get two of your pineapple gelatos, to go? My friend and I have some other things to take care of, but she would *kill* me if I didn't at least let her sample that."

Gregorio clapped his hands; his curly black hair and mustache swaying. "Of course! It will be right out." He hurried away, dodging in and out of his servers and customers. "Frederick! Freddy! I need two pineapple gelatos! Now!"

Daphne nodded. "I get it," she said as Apollo returned his attention to the table. "You granted his prayer, didn't you?"

"Of course. What I was hoping you would no-tice, though, is *how*."

Daphne wrinkled her brow. "What do you mean? You didn't just wave your hand, and, *bam*, suddenly money was coming his way?"

Apollo laughed. "No. I suppose I could have—done the Midas touch for him, have things turn into gold—but that's a childish trick, really. As you get older, you realize two things." He took a drink of his wine, then began enumerating the points on his fin-gers.

"One—doing things like creating gold and jew-els disrupts the economy. Locally, the disruption is heaviest, but enough manipulation can cause an en-tire country's finances to go into ruin."

Daphne tapped her glasses. "I take it you've learned that one the hard way."

Apollo pulled out the collar of his shirt. "Guilty as charged, madam."

"Okay, then what's the second thing?"

"It draws attention, someone suddenly coming into a large amount of wealth. People want to know how, where it happened. Form a pattern, and –"

"And then Crusaders come knocking, wonder-ing where you are."

He nodded. "Exactly so."

Daphne glanced around, then leaned in. "So...if you don't mind me asking..."

Apollo whipped out a smartphone, made a few button presses, and showed the screen to the young woman. Her eyes flicked across the glowing display, growing wider and wider as they moved.

"That...I've never seen..."

"Smart investments. It's easy to do when you can see the future." He checked his watch. "Speaking of which, there's another worship ceremony coming up in three days, at sunset. A large one. Would you like to join me?"

Daphne choked down her *yes*. "I...I would, but I think I should probably get back to school." Apollo raised his eyebrows. "Not that school has anything on traveling the world with the sun god, you understand, but..."

"Of course. It will take you time to adjust, get used to this side of the world. And you have people you wish to connect with, say goodbye to, if necessary. That sort of thing."

Daphne heard the assumption in his words. She leaned forward, her arms crossed on the table. "You don't have to deal with disappointment much, do you?"

Apollo rapped on his forehead. "Prophetic. God of oracles, remember?"

Daphne laughed and shook her head. "I don't know if I could live like that, always able to see the future. Doesn't it get boring, knowing what's going to happen all the time?"

Apollo seemed to consider this; he brought one hand up and held his chin while his eyes looked downward, inward. "No." His gaze came back to Daphne. "Not at all. Not that I don't understand why you would think that it would, but..." He crossed his arms, still considering. "I suppose it's the difference between knowing the ending of a story and hearing the story itself. Just because you know the ending –"

"Doesn't mean that you can't enjoy the journey." The two voices echoed together, and Apollo uncrossed his arms and touched one of Daphne's hands with his own.

Soft, warm, yielding skin, pressed against hers. The taste of him on her lips as she kissed her way down his chest.

She stiffened, pulling her hand away.

"I guess I have to ask, then. Are you manipulating this?" She waved her hands in the air. "Using your foreknowledge to back me into a corner, to do all the right things so I don't have a choice?"

Apollo waited, licked his lips, took a drink from his wineglass. Daphne watched his every movement, her heart thudding in her ears, sweat greasing her palms.

What will he say? Will he even tell me the truth? Do I even want to know?

He put the drink down, met her eyes.

Smiled.

"No."

A combination of relief and irritation broke over her. "Um...why not?"

The shock on his face startled her. "Because it wouldn't be right."

She blinked.

"When I was young, I believed that mortals were beneath me, that my status as a god set me above them in some important, defining way. I meddled in lives, bristled when I was challenged, decided the course of wars." He gazed off into the distance. "It was easy, then, not to see what wrongs I was committing."

His focus came back to Daphne, razor-sharp. "The Trojan War showed me how mistaken I was. I sided against most of my family, chose to defend Troy."

"But you lost." She took a breath. "How did that—"

"Because I got to see the results of our actions." Apollo's eyes were wide, his voice rising in volume. "Thousands, millions dead because of us, because of our pettiness. My sister Eris deceived Hera, Athena, and Aphrodite, casting the world into the Discord that she loved so much. We could have stopped it, but each of us—myself included—was so angry at the slights we perceived that we used the men and women as if they were chess pieces to be discarded at will."

He subsided, returning to a more normal tone. "I watched them all die. I watched Hector—noble, righteous, a man who only wished to protect his homeland—slain because of us. Watched his wife and child murdered because of us. Watched the entire future of a nation vanish."

He turned his head away. "Because of us."

Daphne's lip trembled. "That's horrible. I'm...I'm so sorry."

Apollo nodded. "Since then, I no longer take it upon myself to intervene in human lives unless asked. I may be immortal, but this does not make me better suited to decide the fate of even one man or woman than they are."

The words reached through the protective shell Daphne had spun about her heart. She brought her chair over to the other side of the table, sitting beside him.

He glanced up at her, a faint glimmer of hope playing on his face.

Her lips moved to form words of comfort, of understanding...of respect and admiration.

No.

"What about me?" In an instant, the compassion she felt was choked off, strangled in its bed.

His eyes narrowed, confused. "I don't understand."

"You intervened in my life. Took me away. If you hadn't come back, then I never would have found out my roommate was a cultist psycho. I would have just kept going to class, trying to become a writer, trying to live my life." Tears began to leak down her face. "But now I have to remember, always, what you were, what I've seen...and nothing will ever feel the same anymore."

"Then come with me!" He was earnest now, pleading. "You don't have to forsake what I have to offer you. You can be part of—"

"Part of what? Your fan club? The huge list of conquests?" She caught her voice rising, brought it down to avoid attracting attention. "Part of the regrets of a god who *intervened* one too many times?"

Silence.

"...You are right." Apollo bowed his head. "I was selfish, and I forced myself into your life when I should not have. I shall return you to your campus when you are ready." Apollo stood, waved once more in Gregorio's direction, and put out his hand to help Daphne up.

She didn't take it.

Why are you being such a bitch?

Because he's a goddamn hypocrite, that's why. Says he doesn't change people's lives...what about mine?

"Daphne, I know I have wronged you. I know you are angry." He still held out his hand. "But I will keep my promise. Once I have brought you home, you will never see me again."

The woman's soul seemed torn in two, one rejoicing Apollo's words and the other lamenting. Her stern, pinched face relaxed.

A little.

"No, I'm not being fair. I'm...I'm sorry." She took his hand, ignoring the frisson that went up her spine, and stood. "I don't want to never see you again. Just...just not like that. Okay?"

A small smile. "As you wish."

Chapter Sixteen

Daphne rolled out of bed, stretched, smiled at the alarm clock. 7:54. Six minutes before it went off. "It's going to be a good day."

She switched off the clock and turned on the radio as she shucked her night clothes and slipped into the shower. She sang along with the music as she bathed, finishing up and wrapping herself in a green towel. Brushing her hair out, she walked back into the main portion of her room.

Cassandra was standing in the middle of the dwelling, her hair down, draped over her bowed head, dressed only in a white shift; the clothes swayed with the girl, and Daphne could hear a soft mumbling, sing-song style, coming from Cassandra.

"One, two, looking for you...three, four, can't run anymore..."

Daphne walked toward her friend, putting a hand on her shoulder. "Are you okay, Cassie? Is something wrong?"

The sing-song continued. "Five, six...nothing he predicts...seven, eight, can't see his fate..."

A shiver tore its way down Daphne's spine; her breath caught, and she pulled her hand back to her chest. "Why are you singing? Cassie?"

The room went dark; a quick glance toward the window showed Daphne that the sunlight was no longer coming through it. The glowing disk was covered by a roiling darkness, blotting out the day, and all over the campus, people were gaping up at the sky, pointing, shouting, screaming in fear.

"What's...?" She turned back toward Cassandra, who had not moved, who was still in the same spot, but now, blood was dripping, drip-drip, from her face, pattering on the ground, forming a puddle that the girl's toes were dipping in. The blood was dark, clotted, with small chunks of something floating in the pool.

"Nine, ten, let me tell you again..." Cassandra turned her face toward Daphne. Daphne's eyes went wide, and she hit the wall, scrabbling against it, trying to get away, unable to scream.

"The better to see you with, my dear!"

Where Cassandra's strange white eyes had been, now there were only gouged-out holes, angry, swollen, still bleeding. Cassandra's hands reached out for Daphne, coming closer as she approached.

"They took them, they took them, they took them..."

Daphne found her voice and, before Cassandra's fingers could close on her shoulders, she let loose the scream from her chest.

~~~

"Daphne! Wake up! Are you all right?"

Daphne's limbs flailed, striking steel, faux-leather, flesh. Her eyes danced around like a madwoman's, unable to settle, seeing the environment without seeing. Apollo grabbed hold of her limbs and held them to her. Her head continued to thrash until he caught her eyes with his own.

She stilled, still breathing fast, a runner after a mile-long sprint.

Apollo did not take his eyes off her.

"Sir, is she okay?" came a voice from the seat behind them.

"She'll be fine. I think it was just a bad dream." He still did not look away.

"Hell of a bad dream, man."

Daphne's breathing began to slow, and she could take in the environment around her. She was on a hard seat, near a window. The world outside was moving.
~~~

A bus. They were taking a bus. She was with Apollo, going back to school on a Greyhound.

"*Are* you all right, Daphne?" The god's voice was a murmur—low, intimate, almost whispered in her ear.

Daphne's mouth opened, but nothing came out—*why is my mouth so dry?*—so she settled for nodding. Apollo returned the nod and released her arms.

"I don't know what you were dreaming, but you could have hurt yourself...or anyone else nearby, for that matter."

Daphne's hands dove under her seat and came up with her bottle of Dasani, which she upended and chugged. One of Apollo's eyebrows arched as he watched her down the entire twenty-ounce bottle in about ten seconds. She came back up for air, shaking her head and dropping the bottle into her lap.

"...Very well." Apollo glanced at his watch. "We've got about another half hour or so before we get there." He examined her face. "Are you sure you're all right?"

Daphne rubbed her hands up and down her arms, chilled. "It was awful. Cassandra was...someone had blinded her, torn her eyes out. She was singing. It..." She shook her head and shuddered again. "It was awful."

Apollo searched her face. She watched as his eyes shifted, went from a probing concern to a cautious optimism. "It doesn't look oracular."

"What?" Daphne blinked under his scrutiny. "What do you mean?"

"Prophetic visions and dreams leave behind traces of power. I can see those." A small smile touched his lips. "It means you weren't watching the future, Daphne. You were just having a dream."

Daphne shook her head, rubbed her fingertips into her eyes. "It was so real. I can see her face every time I close my eyes." She turned to Apollo. "Why would I dream something like that?"

The golden god pursed his lips. "Morpheus may have been able to tell you. The ins-and-outs of human dreams are beyond even the gods, except when we influence them, of course." His eyes were piercing, strong. "I would not worry overmuch. You have been through a lot lately. It is only natural that your mind is seeking relief."

Something about Apollo's words sounded off to Daphne's ear, like a song she had heard before, but in a different version. "I wish that it wouldn't seek *that* kind of relief. It's like getting a break from boredom by being thrown out the window."

Apollo laughed. "Such are the mysteries of man and woman." He opened his hands and a gentle glow suffused the air above them. "More complex than those of the sun and moon themselves—we gods are simple compared to you."

Daphne laughed along with him, the sound beginning to dispel the horror that clung to her mind like seaweed. She looked out the window again.

"Besides, you will see her very soon now." Apollo's voice was cheerful. "I'm sure that it will be a relief to get back to a bit of normality, won't it?"

Daphne breathed out through her nose, clouding the window in a fan-pattern for a moment. "Yeah. It'll be nice to see Cassie with her eyes in her head, even if they do look a little weird."

~~~

The two traveled across the campus; the sunlight was dying, the dorms and classroom buildings casting long shadows over the grass. Daphne licked her lips as she and Apollo walked toward the dormitory. Several times she began to speak, but found the words stilled in her throat. No words were exchanged until the pair reached the dormitory building.

She turned to him as they stood on the threshold; students of both genders were passing in and out of the building, and more than a few were giving the youthful deity appraising glances, or throwing unbelieving ones her way. Daphne took a breath to say something.
~~~

Let it out again.

Apollo glanced at the doorway, back to her. "Here you are."

Daphne swallowed and nodded, a hard lump in her throat. *This is good. It'll be good to be away from him for a while, to be able to think without seeing...hearing...smelling...*

"Do you want to come in before you go?"

The words were out of her mouth before she had a chance to examine them or arrest their progress. *He's the god of the arts and creativity, that's all. How can I miss the chance?* She tipped her chin up and met his gaze. "I know you've been there before, but maybe I could take some time to show you the things that I do, normally. Some of my writing. It's nothing like living on Olympus or flying in a flaming chariot, but—"

Apollo put his finger on his lips. "That would be wonderful, Daphne. I'd love to see how you live your life."

She nodded, ignoring the butterflies that were taking up residence in her stomach.

What if he doesn't like it? It's only a rough draft...

"Okay, then." The two headed inside, and the scene closely resembled the rubbernecking of drivers after a bad car accident, with more than one collision occurring as passers-by lost track of where they were going as they stared after the girl and the Greek god.

There were several catcalls as well. "You go, girl!" "Where'd you pick that one up?" "Damn! I want some of that when you're done!"

Daphne hunched her shoulders against the verbal barrage. "Come on. Let's go." She walked a few steps into the hallway, then stopped.

Apollo was not beside her.

She turned. He was standing in the middle of the entryway, his eyes wide, his nostrils flaring. At his sides, his hands were clenched into angry fists, and heat warped the air around his shoulders.

"Still your tongues." His voice was low, seething with suppressed anger, a solar flare just beneath the surface of his words. "You demean yourselves, and you demean me and my friend. The first I can forgive, but not the last."

Murmurs ran through the crowd. Several people laughed. One, a tall, ripped young man with dark curls and tattoos on his arms, approached Apollo. He stood three inches shorter than the god, and stuck his chest out to press against the tailored clothes Apollo wore.

"Hey, man, what the hell's your problem? People are just talkin', you know? No reason to get all pissed off at us just for having a little fun." He looked past Apollo's shoulder at Daphne, and his mouth curled in a lascivious smile. "You know, sweetheart, if you want to ditch the blond, I'm in room 221."

Apollo took a step back, leveling the full power of his eyes at the man. "If lust is all that consumes you, rutting beast, so be it." The quality of the light in the room changed, as if Daphne were viewing it through smoky glass.

"You have affronted me with your words and your actions. As such, I level judgment upon you—that which has consumed you will no longer be within your grasp. Your rutting, your indiscriminate lusts, will eat at you, unfulfilled, until you go mad."

Daphne tugged at his clothes. "Let's go."

Apollo's face was still angry, set. "I cannot allow—"

She put a hand on his shoulder, pulled. "Don't forget Troy."

He stopped in his tracks, his eyes darting and brow furrowing. "...Yes. You are right." He brought his eyes back up to the tattooed man. "Go in peace. Your follies shall have their own consequences."

Then he turned, heading up the stairs with Daphne following behind.

"Thank you." He did not turn, but his pace slowed once he reached the second floor.

"You looked like you were going to kill him." She came up to his side and assessed his expression. He still had a few anger lines marking his face, but there was also a small smile playing on his lips.

"Kill him? No. Give him a pair of donkey testicles, maybe."

Daphne's eyebrows rose to the top of her forehead and she erupted in laughter. "Come on," she managed, "we can still go back."

His smile grew. "No. I'd rather enjoy myself examining your work."

She gave his shoulder a friendly shove and they resumed their journey. "Come on, you can't tell me that in ancient Greece you never got a catcall or two?"

"Nothing so vulgar." They arrived at the entrance to Daphne's room, and she turned her key in the lock. "Often, they would –"

Her fingers moved to the light switch, flicked it on.

Nothing happened.

"That's weird." Daphne stepped into her room, moving the switch a few more times with the same result. Apollo followed behind.

"What's wrong?"

Daphne began to turn away from the fixture. "I don't know. Light switch isn't working. Maybe –"

The door slammed shut behind them. Both whirled around to face the center of the room and the doorway.

One Templar stood behind the door, his hand still on it. Another emerged from the bathroom, and a third stood up from the floor beside the bed. Two brandished swords, curved with runic script, and the last moved to block the window, holding an ornate bow that twinkled red in the sunlight.

"There is no escape this time, Apollo."

Daphne's eyes were wide as she stepped forward. "...Chloe? Is that you?"

The girl lowered her hood to reveal her blonde hair and sad smile. "Hello, Daphne. I'm sorry to see you here. I had hoped to spare you when I took your memory." She turned her gaze to the god at Daphne's side. "The chase is over, abomination. In the name of God, you will be destroyed and the Earth cleansed of your influence."

Apollo snarled, his suit shimmering into the silver-and-gold armor plating he wore in combat. His golden bow materialized in his hands, and he aimed it at Chloe. "I do not know how you surprised me today, woman, but I will not be defeated easily."

Chloe showed no concern for the silver-tipped arrow leveled at her chest. "Oh, I believe you will, Apollo. You see..." In a single smooth motion, she pivoted, raised her bow, nocked an arrow, and loosed it at Daphne. The arrowhead was a dark, sullen metal, and it struck the young woman before she had time to do more than begin to open her mouth and scream.

"Daphne!" Apollo turned, dropping his own weapon and cradling her in his arms as she fell, eyes closed. The wound in her chest closed over the arrowhead, leaving behind a foul-smelling smoke, and she groaned, stirring, her eyes still shut.

Sun-fire erupted from Apollo's golden skin, scorching the floor around him. The blast of light left shadows on the paint like those after a nuclear explosion. He stood, Daphne in his arms, and turned back to face his assailants.

"If she dies, not even your god will save you, woman." His voice crackled with power, bouncing off the walls and floor. "You will serve an eternity of torment in Tartarus for this."

Chloe laughed. "Don't you even recognize your own family's things?" She held up the bow for Apollo to see, and the solar fury dissipated like it was never there.

"No..."

The Templar's smirk was cruel and cutting. "Yes. Eros' bow, the lead arrow shot into her heart. When she awakens and sees you –"

"Her soul will shun me, fear me, as before." All the courage and confidence had been sapped from his voice, and he seemed to crumble inward. "Why have you done this?"

Chloe nodded, and the two other Templars advanced on Apollo, swords at the ready. "I know that you love her. We found that out ourselves. I also know that, out of all of your family, you are the greatest threat—you have watched us, observed us, know how we fight. You could probably escape from here like you did before, if we gave you the time to compose yourself."

Her blonde hair swayed as she nodded toward the woman he carried in his arms. "But I don't think that you want to go on living your immortal life knowing that you cannot see her again."

Apollo's eyes raised. "If she sees another man, then the curse is lifted. I –"

"No." Chloe shook her head. "We've had a lot of time with your family's relics, and our leaders have prayed to God for assistance. The arrows are now attuned to a particular target. She will hate you, and only you, the very next time she thinks of you." She slung the weapon over her shoulder. "Unfortunately, she won't forget you this time. That didn't work out before. Instead, she'll remember everything, but wonder why she was ensorcelled." A shrug. "Nothing you can do."

Apollo kissed Daphne's forehead, then laid her on her bed. The Templars tracked his movements with their weapons.

"Very well. You have taken my family, and you have taken my love." His hands bunched into fists, then relaxed. "There is nothing left for me here."

Chloe nodded again, and one of the Templars brought out a pair of manacles, laced with holy writings and symbols of power. He locked them around Apollo's wrists.

"How right you are, abomination. How right you are."

Chapter Seventeen

Daphne.

Daphne opened her eyes. For several seconds, the world around her was blurred, indistinct; she brought up a hand to wipe the water from her vision.

It did not go. In fact, her hand was dripping wet, as were her clothes. She sat upright.

Beside her sat the water nymph, the naiad, she had seen that day in Publix. Her eyes were deep sea-green, with no pupils. Daphne's head had been resting on the naiad's lap, and she had been caressing Daphne's forehead, leaving behind a trail of warmth and moisture.

Daphne began to stand, but the naiad placed a hand on her chest. Soothing calm radiated from that touch.

"Please do not struggle, Sister. You are safe now."

Daphne stilled, her eyes dancing around as her sight cleared. "What happened?"

Another warm caress, this one on her cheek. "I had hoped you would tell me."

The memories were long in coming; they seemed clouded, immersed deeply in muddy water or obscured by the leaves of a forest canopy. "I...I was with Apollo. We were in my dorm room. We were talking, and then –"

Her eyes widened and turned, staring her in the face. "Then they came for him. Chloe and her people were there. I need to –"

"Daphne, stop." The nymph took Daphne's head in her hands. "Look at yourself."

Daphne looked down and gasped; sticking out of her chest was a great arrow. Its crystal shaft sparked and pulsed with power, and the edges of the barbed arrowhead were visible under the skin. She touched the projectile, then looked back at the naiad, confused.

"What...what is this? What happened to me?"

The nymph took Daphne's hand. "You were struck in the heart by Eros' bow. The lead arrow was used, meaning that–"

"The next man I see...I would hate." Daphne shuddered, but the naiad shook her head in negation.

"This arrow was ensorcelled by powerful magic. It was made for one purpose—that you would despise the Sun himself. No other."

"Chloe...Chloe wanted me to hate Apollo? Why?"

Her companion stood. "I cannot know. What I do know is that the arrow is still within you, which means that something has gone wrong with Eros' power." Her sea-green eyes lingered on the weapon. "Tell me...*do* you hate Apollo?"

Daphne considered; in her mind, she replayed every scene, every memory. She watched him watching her from her window, revisited their first real meeting in her room. The chariot ride. The sight of Olympus. His smile as she drifted off to sleep after they made love, and the confusion in the wake of her rage.

His apologies, the attempts to make amends. In each memory, she lingered over his face, his laugh, his kindness.

"No." She shook her head. "No, I don't."

"Then you are in great danger." The nymph took two steps toward the woman. "If the arrow cannot bring you sorrow, cannot fulfill its purpose, then the magic could become corrupt within you. Like a disease."

Daphne recoiled. "What...what can I do?"

"We must remove the arrow."

"You mean...pull it out? Won't that hurt?"

The naiad nodded. "Yes. It may take away some part of your heart as it goes. You may lose consciousness. You may die. If you do not, however, then there is no hope for you at all, and you will succumb to the corrupt infection soon enough."

Daphne wrapped her hands around the crystalline arrow. Even touching it caused searing pain to erupt within her chest, and she bit her lip to stifle the cry. She closed her eyes and Apollo's face emerged from the darkness.

Pull it out, Daphne, he had asked. *Don't leave me again. Pull it out.*

Her grip tightened and her jaw set against the pain.

It doesn't matter if it's magic that made him want me. I won't let magic make me hate him.

She pulled.

Not again.

~~~

The man who stood beside the laurel tree was not as radiant as the one who had pursued her, but his face was kind and compassionate. His back held a pair of great wings, like an angel, and his eyes were troubled. He also held a bow, although his was made of crystal, and he put a hand on the bark of the tree.

His touch did not burn Daphne's face, and she relaxed within her woody prison.
~~~

"I am sorry." He shook his head and dropped his hand. "I was foolish. Easily goaded by my cousin, Apollo." The young man sat, looking up at the tree. "He claimed that I was not worthy of my weapon, you see, because the bow belonged to him and his sister well before I was born."

He fitted an arrow, this one tipped with gold, to his bow and drew back the string, aiming at nothing in particular. "Apollo can cure or kill with his bow. He can cause a pestilence that slays a city, or bring the blessings of health to the same. Artemis can pick off a man miles away with her arrows, or trap a god with a shot through both of his ankles." He laughed, and his laugh was rich, sensual.

He held the bow up for Daphne to see. "My power is different. With my bow, I make men and women lust for each other or repelled by one anoth-er. He challenged my strength, and, like a child, I had to prove that I was as strong as he, in my way. I struck him through the heart with the golden ar-row." He closed his eyes and pursed his lips. "And, when he saw you, I sent the opposite, the lead, into your own heart, that you would never submit to him."

Anger rose within Daphne. *How could you? Why would you?* Her branches moved and leaves whispered, but she could not truly speak.

He nodded as if he could hear her admonitions. "Exactly. How could I? You were an immortal creature, Daphne. And my intervention has denied you your life, your happiness. I have proven myself as childlike as my cousin claimed." He sighed. "I acted below my station, and I am truly sorry."

He stood and, once more, placed a hand on the bark. "I cannot undo what has been done, Daphne. You no longer have a heart, and my power cannot affect what is not there. Instead, I give you a promise. When it is time, when the world is ready once more, you will live again, to have the life that my rashness has stolen from you."

"You realize the cost of your promise, Eros, do you not?"

The young god turned toward the sound of the woman's voice behind him. There were three, wrapped in robes of shimmering white, of different ages. The one who had spoken was the youngest, barely an adult, with long, blonde hair and knitting a thread. That thread was held by the second, a black-haired, mature woman who was measuring it by lengths before passing it to the third. The third woman, an old crone whose eyes were clouded by cataracts and whose face resembled a mountainside, held a rusted, pitted pair of shears, and the thread fell within them, moving, waiting for the cut which would sever it.

Eros nodded. "It is my duty that I fulfill now. I have wronged both this nymph and my cousin, Apollo. I would make it right."

The middle woman spoke. "Then it falls that you will be forgotten. Your image remembered by few, at the end of days. Changed. Contorted, such that you will never be recognized. This is the cost for what you ask of us."

Eros closed his eyes. "Very well, Moirai. Let it be so. If I renege, may I be forced to drink from the Styx, as commanded by Zeus."

The last, the crone, nodded. "Very well. Then by our power, I place this thread into abeyance." The youngest of the three stopped her spinning and released the thread; it floated from their grasp and drifted toward the oldest, who looped it around her arm and hung it over her shoulder.

"Is it done?"

"Not yet, son of Aphrodite." The young woman smiled. "Clotho must prepare the thread to receive the second life she will have."

"What do you –"

The shears closed, and a small portion off the edge of the strand fell to the ground. The tree withered, its leaves crumbling to dust and its branches crisping as if it had been in the sun for months.

"Now we can splice her new life onto the old, you see." Clotho cackled. "Only a cut thread can be connected to another."

Eros nodded, and touched the trunk of the dead tree one more time. "Goodbye, Daphne. I hope that you can forgive me in your next life."

Chapter Eighteen

Again, Daphne opened her eyes, but this time things were different.

"Sister? Are you all right?"

She stood, her hand moving to the space on her chest where the arrow had been. It was out, lying on the ground beside her feet.

"Sister?"

Daphne breathed in, inhaling the aroma of the plants and trees, the lake and the flowers around her. Her mind quivered at the edge of madness as she felt two separate but connected existences being twined together like spliced rope. Where before, her memories started at four or five years old, now they went back many thousands of years, the legacy of an immortal existence that had once been hers.

Been hers before Apollo and Eros. Before their challenge. Rage pulsed in her chest, and she could feel the world responding to it. Thorns lengthened, flowers dwindled, and tree canopies thickened to blot out the sunlight.

"Sister!"

Daphne turned to the naiad. The water creature's eyes were wide in terror, flicking around Daphne's form. A forest-green aura, rich, powerful, and deep, was pulsing around the young woman, and the grasses were writhing beneath her. The snakes in the treetops above the pool increased their sibilant song, nearly drowning out the other noises around.

Daphne saw what her rage was doing, but the first part of her life, the new part, the one which was immeasurably older and more experienced than the other, was *angry,* and was ready to take that anger out on the world. Images of Apollo, chasing after her, that inhuman lust in his eyes –

Stop it!

The other voice, the other half, the life that was Daphne Gianakos, young college student from Maine, stood up.

If you let yourself do this, you're worse than they ever were. A monster. Is that what you want to be?

"They deserve it." Her words came from gritted teeth, but the aura was faltering, weakening. "They need to be punished for what they did, for what –"

It's been centuries. Things have changed. He's lived for so long with everyone else dead. Isn't that enough? You're alive.

"What life is this?" She cut the air with her hand. "Condemned to a world polluted by idiocy, divided amongst the faithless?"

I won't let you hurt him.

A pause.

I won't hurt him. Let it go.

And she did. The two halves of her psyche joined with an almost audible *click*, and the power she had drawn dissipated in a huge thunderclap that emanated out from the pool and shook the trees.

"I'm all right." She looked up at the terrified naiad. "I'm all right...Sister."

The water nymph walked over to Daphne, looked into her eyes, then embraced her. Daphne returned the hug, then stepped back, holding the other by the shoulders.

"We need to help Apollo. He's in danger."

The naiad nodded. "But how? I've heard about the ones who have him. How are we supposed to fight someone who was able to slay Zeus? Ares?"

"We don't have enough information." Daphne frowned. "We need to find Cassandra."

"Who is that?"

Daphne smiled. "A Seer. And a friend."

"Do you know where she is?"

She nodded. "Yes. And I think she'll be happy to help us, once we tell her what's going on."

The naiad drew herself up. "All right. I'm ready. My name is Climethea, and I will not let the Sun God die if I can prevent it."

Daphne laughed. "Let's not jump into this too fast, okay? We don't need to go getting ourselves into honorable deaths just yet."

~~~

"Cassandra? Cassie? Are you here?"

Daphne turned the key she had gotten from the R.A. in the lock of Cassandra's door. "She said Cassie hasn't been back here for a while." The lock clicked and Daphne nodded at Climethea. "Let's go."

The door opened without a sound. Climethea was huddled behind the more confident woman, clutching at the edges of her own dress, her skin and clothing mostly transparent to light. "Wait...what if they're waiting for us?"

"We don't have time to worry about that." The door swung open and light flowed from the hallway into the room beyond. "Besides, Cassie is my friend. I need to make sure that she's okay." Visions of the nightmare tried to crowd in through her mind's eye—Cassandra standing in her room, blood and tissue floating in a puddle before her, her eye sockets empty, hollow—but she shook her head and
~~~

pushed away the images, turning her attention to the search ahead.

Both women gasped.

The room had been trashed. The contents of Cassandra's closet were tossed on the bed, shredded, pulled open; the mattress itself had been flipped and cut apart. The lights were smashed, the lamps broken apart so that small Smurf noses and ears lay scattered around the floor.

Daphne stepped in, edging around the debris. "It doesn't look like they left anything, does it?" She looked up at the ceiling, where the remnants of a mobile, a solar system design, still hung.

"What do you think they were looking for?" Climethea's voice trembled, like her hands, and she hovered near the door, a bird ready to fly at the first hint of danger.

Daphne reached up for the ruin of the Sun model, cracked in half. "I don't know." She let it go, and it swung in a lazy arc on its wire. "But whatever it was, I think it would be best if we found it."

"They probably already got whatever it was." The naiad's flesh was solid now, but very pale. "We should probably go."

Daphne shook her head. "Cassie was a Seer. She knew things before they were going to happen, like Apollo. She would have seen this coming."

"Then why –"

"Why did she get caught?" Daphne laughed and moved the bed to the side, sifting through some of the wreckage. "Beats me. I think she was a fatalist—can't change the future once you see it, that sort of thing." She cocked an eyebrow and stood up again, quiet.

"Wait...that doesn't make sense."

Climethea looked up from her huddled position near the doorframe. "What doesn't, Sister?"

Daphne began to pace the room, her words coming faster and faster. "Cassie was a Seer. You and I know that the Fates are...were...I don't know which, but they were in charge of the future. They spun it, they wove it, they knew it."

Climethea nodded, her eyes narrowed. "...So?"

"They could change their minds. They did for me. They did for Heracles. They did at Zeus' behest several times, and many more he asked and they refused him." Daphne sank to the ground in the center of the room.

"She had to know." Her eyes widened, and she caught her breath. "She did know. She told me that, once, that it was because people didn't believe her that she couldn't help them, couldn't save them with her warnings. She did know."

Climethea crept closer, keeping low to the ground like her companion. "So...if she were going to hide something because she knew they were coming—"

"She might have known I was going to follow!" Daphne's head turned right and left, her expression manic. "She would have left me, would have given me a signal, a sign, something. A clue."

"Daphne, calm down. You can't think if you're hyperventilating. Breathe."

Daphne's head shake fanned her red hair out in waves. "No. No time." She ran her hands through her hair. "Where is it, Cassie? Where wouldn't they look?"

Her friend's brow furrowed. "I don't think there's anywhere here, Daphne. Look; they even broke the television set looking for whatever it was."

There was a moment of silence.

"Of course. It's not here." Daphne stood, a wide-eyed stare coming to rest on the naiad. "Why would it be here? If she knew what was coming, she wouldn't have left it *here*. It would be somewhere else." The smile spread across her face like ice crystallizing on a lake. "Somewhere that hidden messages could be found."

Climethea smiled as well. "You know where it is, don't you?"

Without another word, Daphne ran out of Cassandra's dorm room and hit the stairwell. Thirty more seconds and she was unlocking the door to her own place, diving toward her bookbag. A few more moments and she had extracted her copy of the Holy Bible. She began to leaf through it, then shook her head and turned it upside down, shaking it several times.

A folded piece of paper fell out.

"Got you!" Climethea plucked it from the floor and opened it, scanning the text.

"What does it say?"

She licked her lips and her brow knotted. "I don't understand." She held the note out for Daphne to read. "It doesn't make any sense to me."

Daphne,

Hope is not lost. Do you remember what I told you at the beginning of the year? When we first met?

"She told that my life would pour onto the dirt...from my heart." Her hand went to her chest.

Climethea frowned. "Didn't that...didn't that already happen? When you pulled the arrow out?"

Daphne bit her lip. "I don't know."

Yes. Surviving means that you have a chance...and so do the rest of us. But only if you act quickly.

Daphne's breath caught in her chest, and her heart felt like it weighed thousands of pounds.

If the Golden Man falls, the world will end, Daphne. It will end in fire, and it will end in blood, and there will be a woman standing amongst it all, covered in the offerings of the survivors, coated in crimson red. I don't know who she is, but she will end him. And she will do it soon. This I have seen.

"Then what can I do?" Daphne spoke as if Cassandra were present to answer her questions. "What can I *do*?"

Follow his light, Daphne. Follow his light. It will always lead to him. I wish it didn't have to be this way. I love you. And I forgive you.—Cassie

She shook her head. *Forgive me for what?*

"Follow his light?" Climethea rubbed her temples with the tips of her fingers. "What does that mean?"

Daphne let the letter slip from her fingers. "Apollo's light." She nodded, her face set. "Sunlight, of course. We need to follow the sun."

Climethea was silent for a moment, and Daphne could see the naiad working out the connections in her own mind, confirming Daphne's intuitive leap. Then she frowned and wrapped her arms around the former dryad.

"You...you're going to save him, right?" Her arms tightened. "You won't let this happen, will you?"

Daphne pushed herself away from the girl's clutches. "Hey. What's wrong?"

Climethea's face was bloodless; even the sea-green of her eyes had paled.

"I know that this is terrible, but –"

"You don't understand. You didn't have to live through it all." Climethea hunched her back, cradling her hands in her lap, rubbing her palm with her thumb. "He was the last one, Daphne. The only god left. The only one who came, the only one who remembered the stories." Her eyes came back up, radiant pools shimmering in the waning light. "He was the only one left to remind me of the way things had been. He was the only one I saw for hundreds of years." She reached for Daphne's hands, holding them tight in her own. "You can't know what it was like, being alone for so long, afraid they would find me. Terrified, Daphne; I was so afraid that they would take me away...or take him away."

"Shhh." Daphne tried to remove her hands, to comfort her companion, but Climethea held tight. "Hey...let go."

"Then they had him, Daphne. They took him away, captured him." She leaned forward, and her volume climbed. Tears poured from her eyes, but she kept speaking. "They came to me and asked me to help them. So that he could be free again." She bowed her head. "So that he could be free again."

Daphne stopped struggling against the naiad's iron fingers. Her eyes began to scan the room, alighting on the window. The sun was descending in the sky, and a sliver of the sun disk was visible at the top of the window.

Keep her talking. "What did they ask you to do?"

Climethea shook her head as if she didn't want to respond, but the words came, choked in her sobs. "They...they wanted me to find out if you were affected by the arrow. Eros' bow. They said that the Lethe powder didn't work on you and they weren't sure if this would, so they asked me to watch. They told me that, if you went after Apollo, I was to watch you, follow you, see what you were going to do." Another sob. "And then I was supposed to ambush you. Kill you."

Half of the sun could now be seen; it was swollen red. *Like blood.*

"Then why didn't you do it, Climethea? Why didn't you just kill me?"

"I...I..." Climethea shuddered. "I don't know. I didn't want to. I've missed you so much, you and all the others. I didn't know what to do, so I just followed you." Another shudder, then she straightened and looked Daphne in the eye.

My God.

Within the sea-green of the naiad's gaze, Daphne could see a roiling storm, a hurricane of power. *What is she going to do?*

"I'm sorry, Sister, but I need him. I have survived these centuries without you; I would not have survived without him. I need him." Climethea's eyes flashed and her hands began to bear down, pressing on Daphne's bones and flesh with terrible force even as the water nymph leaned forward and kissed her on the forehead.

Daphne's eyes were watering from the pain, but she cast another glance at the window. The sun was now fully visible, a huge, fat, red circle in the sky.

Despite her agony, she smiled in the face of her attacker, who faltered for a moment.

"I...I'm sorry, Sister, but I won't let you stop me." She pushed forward, forcing her arms ahead through the pain.

Climethea shook her head and pushed back. "You don't have the power to stop me. Not caught off guard." She began to press Daphne backward, on her knees, toward the floor. "Goodbye –"

Daphne let her muscles go limp. The sudden lack of resistance caused Climethea to stumble, taking several large steps to keep her balance, ending up with her stomach against the windowsill and her forehead pressed against the glass. Daphne sprung back to her feet as the naiad turned around.

The hurricane eyes did not have time to widen before Daphne launched herself over the other girl's head, eyes fixed on the sun. It seemed to fill the whole sky, wavering in the atmosphere, and her eyes burned to watch.

She broke through the glass and began to fall, letting the disk consume her field of vision. For a moment, there was nothing but that crimson monstrosity—no trees, no sky, no ground.

Apollo.

The wind rushed past her ears, and she could feel the ground approaching. Time seemed to slow down, giving her the chance to appreciate each second of life she had left.

Daphne.

She heard a distant thundering, the sound of something strong pounding against the ground over and over again.

The sound of stallions.

Chapter Nineteen

Apollo.

The god's eyes snapped open, flashing gold light in the darkness of his cell. The room was sealed tight and warded against his powers with holy symbols, and for days he had drifted in and out of dreamless sleep, the murmur of unanswered prayers his only companion.

"...Daphne?" His skin began to glow, banishing the oppressive void and illuminating the inside of the room—small, 10 paces to a side, and barren of furnishings. He stood from the corner he had huddled in and cast his senses outward.

His heart stopped, fear gripping it in an unyielding fist.

In his mind's eyes, he could see her. His love was falling, her arms and face cut in a dozen places by shards of glass, the red fluid streaming as she plummeted downward. Her face was turned toward him, tears shimmering, and her eyes were unafraid.

She was praying to him.

Why is she praying to me? She should...she should despise me.

Apollo bent his will, calling on his divinity. The wards in the room enclosed him, compressing him, but still he summoned his power until he was a supernova contained within an aluminum can.

He could see the ground rushing toward her. She was not flinching, not bringing her arms up to shield herself.

I will not fail her. The room began to tremble, the walls shaking under the weight of the power contained within. *I will not.*

"DAPHNE!"

His will and voice exploded outward as one, rending the wards and tearing the roof and walls from their moorings. He fell to his knees, his light guttering, his strength dissipating as men and women in white and red uniforms came running.

His eyes closed, but not before a smile lifted the corners of his mouth.

Fly, Daphne.

~~~
~~~

The Templar saluted his Knight-Commander. "The abomination has been moved to an examination room. He is completely powerless now—the explosion that destroyed his cell seems to have drained the remains of his energy."

Chloe nodded, bringing one foot up to rest on the opposite knee. "It will take time for him to recover, according to the Seer. I will begin at once." She waved a hand, and the Templar brought his fist to his heart, bowed, and turned to walk out.

When the room was clear, a grin began to spread across Chloe's face. Small at first, it moved from gentle amusement to a cruel, cutting blade.

"It'll be over soon, won't it?" She rose from her seat, rolling her head on her neck and stretching out the stiffness in her limbs. "Just one more to go, and then, we're done."

She stopped opposite one of the many mirrors that lined the Headquarters' walls. Gazing into her own eyes, she leaned forward, running a finger across the curve of her jaw.

"Poor Apollo." A chuckle escaped her lips. "Isolation has blinded him, I suppose. Should I tell him? What's going to be more fun?"

~~~

Daphne grasped the edge of the sun-chariot and used it to pull herself up. The two stallions were
~~~

snorting, restless, and the reins were draped over the front, waiting to be held. A quarter-mile below them, the campus seemed quiet and still as night stole in.

"Hey, boys." Daphne's voice cracked, and she swallowed before trying again. "I...Thank you for saving me."

One of the horses stopped pawing the air and turned his head toward her. The broad nose dipped down in an equine nod, then came back up. His eyes stayed on her.

Her hand began to move toward the reins, then she shook her head and closed her fist. "I'm not going to try to command you." The silence was heavy. "Just...we need to save Apollo. Your master is in danger." She leaned toward the stallions, across the front of the carriage. "Do you understand me? He's been trapped, and I don't know where he is. Cassie said you'd know what to do, that you could—"

The chariot lurched forward as the horses lunged. The wheels began to trace out their lines of fire across the sky once more, and Daphne clutched the sides to keep her feet as it accelerated. Up and up they went before turning and streaking through the heavens.

The wind was powerful, blowing Daphne's hair and face, stinging, and she ducked down behind the wall of the chariot to shield herself from the worst of it. As the horses ran, the sun-disk which had dipped below the horizon began to come back into view; they were chasing it, chasing the sun west across the sky.

This isn't quite as much fun alone. "Hey, guys? Not to complain or anything, but I don't suppose that there's any way we could roll up the windows or whatever, is there?"

No answer. *I guess they don't talk.* Her eyes watered, and she wiped the buildup of moisture away with her right hand. When it came back down, her pinky finger brushed against the reins.

The chariot was in full flame now, banishing the cold from the upper atmosphere. The horses' movements became erratic; they strayed to one side, then the other, then dipped down like a meteor descending from space. As Daphne peeked down, she could see the ground below rushing up toward them, a lake and farmland.

The trees and grass were blackening like branches in a fire, the earth cracking as the moisture was sucked out of it. Within moments, the lake began to boil, and the plants to smoke.

Oh my God. Daphne clutched at the chariot edge as she looked upon the devastation that followed the chariot's path as it straightened out and continued its flight. *We're burning the Earth.*

Squinting her eyes against the blistering wind, she looked forward. Rushing toward them was a city—large buildings stretching to the sky, cars and highways, under- and overpasses.

And they were about to die, burned up by the Sun's heat.

Shit shit shit! Daphne stood up and gripped the reins, calling out to the horses. "I'm sorry, boys!"

She pulled up.

It was like pulling a three hundred pound weight with one finger. The stallions did not change course, burning ever onward.

Daphne closed her eyes, trying to remember the story Apollo had referenced. *One person had tried to control the chariot...and he failed.*

Apollo's own son. She refocused her vision; the city was now only a few miles away, a gleaming gem in the path of the destructive missile that was head-ing its way. *Then there's no way I can do it. I'm not strong enough. If Apollo's son wasn't strong enough, how can I be?*

Her eyes lit up. *Maybe it's not about strength.*

She tied the reins off, then stretched out a hand. A soft green glow began to move outward, sparkling, reaching.

And then it formed into an apple tree branch, complete with ripe red fruit dangling in front of and above the horses' heads.

The stallions perked up, reaching their heads up to try to snag one of the tasty red fruits, but the branch stayed out of their reach. They curved upward, chasing the elusive treats.

I guess that being a dryad does have a few advantages. Daphne couldn't stop smiling as the horses began to climb, taking the chariot with them, bringing its terrible heat away from the Earth and the people on it. As they rose, she kept an eye on the ground below. *I doubt we'd actually freeze the world by getting too far away, but better safe than sorry.*

When the landscape below once again resembled what it had looked like at the beginning of her journey, Daphne allowed the fruit branch to bend down, leading the horses on a straight course—streaking west toward the sun.

It did not take long. Within twenty minutes, in a strange display that would not have been out of place in a low-budget time-travel movie, the sun had crawled backward across the sky and now stood at full noon position.

"All right, boys!" The apples hoisted up again, and the stallions' steps followed suit, bringing the chariot in line with the glowing orb in the sky. "Time to find –"

The light cut out.

All motion ceased.

Daphne's blood froze in her veins. *It's like the tree. Dark, trapped like the tree. God, no.*

Daphne put her hands out in the total darkness, praying she would not find herself imprisoned in wood—instead, she felt the metal of the chariot under her fingers, but it was cold, and that cold began to spread. She huddled in on herself, bunching her clothes and rubbing her upper arms against the sudden chill.

"Now what?" She reached into her pocket for her phone. Pressing the power button was difficult with her hands shaking, but the soft glow of the screen brought warmth to banish the fear growing in her heart.

"Good old technology." A few swipes had the menu page for the light application ready; she turned the device outward, towards the darkness. "Well, I guess it's not –"

The light flashed on, and Daphne screamed, her entire body recoiling from the sight before her, her hand losing its grip and dropping the phone into the abyss.

She was thankful for this.

They're all dead. The image was burned in her brain—bodies as far as the eye could see and the light could reach—mutilated, eviscerated, teeth shattered and skulls opened. Some decayed to skeletons, but most with flesh still on them.

Daphne gagged once, twice, then lost the battle and threw her head over the edge of the chariot, her choking spasms sending the evidence of her revulsion down after her four-hundred-dollar phone.

"Why have you come?"

Daphne screamed, retreating from the edge of the chariot and curling into a defensive position on its floor, arms wrapped about her knees. The voice was low, sibilant, and Daphne recognized it as that of Lachesis, the Moira who had measured her life span before Eros made his deal with them. It was a soft sound, but echoed around the girl, giving the impression of a dark concert hall or cavern.

"We know why she is here, sister." The gentle, soothing voice of the maiden Clotho spoke up from Daphne's left. "We have spun the thread of her life well. She seeks to rescue the son of mighty Zeus. She would free Apollo from his imprisonment."

Daphne pulled herself to her feet. "Yes! He's been trapped, and I need—"

She was cut off by the third sister, Atropos, speaking from her right. Her rusty shriek caught Daphne off guard. "All things die. Even gods die, girl. Why should we interfere in this?"

"Because...because it's not right!" She moved her face back and forth between the apparent locations of the three sisters, addressing them all. "You stand for balance, for the natural order. How is it the natural order that servants of Jehovah have killed the entire pantheon of your gods? How is that the way it should be?"

"She does not know what she is saying." Clotho once again, closer now. "She is unaware of the beginning, of how all this came about."

Daphne's eyebrows came together. "Wait...what?" Light-illusions began to dance in the omnipresent darkness, making the girl imagine she could see shapes within it. "What do you mean, the beginning?"

Lachesis's voice was also nearer to the chariot. "What does that matter to us? We measure fate and destiny, we do not apportion it. That is given to something higher than even we."

Daphne turned her head toward Lachesis, hurling her words into the black. "Then why am I alive? If you don't interfere in destiny, why did you bring me back? Why is this the 'right time?'" She began to cry and sank back into the chariot. "Why am I alive at all, then?"

A flash of light, akin to a thunderbolt, lit up the scene for a moment. The field of corpses was crawling, infested with beetles, lice, crawling through eyes and mouths, worms and caterpillars devouring flesh.

Then it was gone.

A squealing chuckle, the repeated sound of metal grating against metal. "Well said, mortal being. My sisters pretend at high-and-mighty directives, but I know where the power truly lies." A loud *snip,* sounding as if it had come from right next to her head, made Daphne jump. "It lies within these."

Snip.

"What do you want?" Daphne tried to still the quavering in her voice, wiping the tears from her eyes. "What will it take for you to help me?"

She could hear the disdain in Clotho's voice. "The woman offers us a trade."

Lachesis gave a soft laugh. "What does she have in her life that we could possibly want, sister? We are forgotten, nothing."

"We exist only to maintain the balance. We require nothing from you."

Daphne shook her head. "There must be something. What if..." She hesitated.

Clotho's whisper hissed in her ear. "What if...?"

The young woman swallowed. "What if...what if I promised to do something for you? A favor. Anything you wanted, whenever you asked." Her head bowed and her voice lowered. "Would you help me then?"

There was a moment of silence before Clotho replied. "You swear this, sworn on the river Styx, the unbetrayable oath of the gods? When we call, you will answer?"

Daphne nodded, clutching a hand to her heart. "I will."

"Done!" The chorus of the three voices crashed upon her, and she buckled under the force. Around her wrist, a fine chain materialized, and she could, for the first time since arriving in this place, feel the chariot beginning to move, feel wind on her face again.

"In order to save The Shining One, you must understand what has come before." The darkness began to fade, a muddled grey instead of pure black. "You must watch the events unfold, that you may act accordingly."

The grey began to break up and moisture tickled Daphne's senses. She could see the chariot and the horses, but they were wrapped in a thick fog. The droplets were chill, and steam flowed from the stallions as they pulled upward. She peeked over the shield provided by the front of the chariot, squinting her eyes against the water and the wind.

The light brightened as the chariot continued its ascent, and Daphne looked around, seeing only more of the grey mist surrounding her. *I think...I think we're in a cloud.*

At that moment, the horses burst through the cottony surface, and the sudden burst of light forced Daphne's eyes closed for several seconds. When she was able to open them again, she shook her head in disbelief.

It's...it's Olympus. Her eyes flicked across the landmarks that Apollo had shown her, the places they had sat and talked. The chariot circled the great mountaintop, and she could see that, this time, the city was not empty. Instead, a myriad of creatures moved about within and above the buildings, and the great forge of Hephaestus poured smoke into the air.

I guess no one told him about global warming, did they? Daphne smirked as she recreated the apple branch to guide the horses in closer. *I wonder if they're going to be able to see me, if this is real or not.*

The fires of the chariot and stallions dimmed as they approached the wide-open gates of Olympus. A single satyr, a creature resembling a half-goat, half-man, stood watch, welcoming all those who entered and waving farewell to those who left. He had a thin, flute-like instrument in one hand and a bunch of grapes in the other.

One smooth landing later and they were gliding down the seamless Olympian streets. Daphne looked at each immortal that they passed.

None turned to look at her.

Guess it's a vision, then. She relaxed and allowed herself to absorb the happenings around her. Satyrs and nymphs were laughing and dancing, and the giggling told Daphne that they might be thinking about what would come after. Athletes competed against one another in a vast amphitheater.

As she passed the entrance to the arena, Daphne saw something that caused her to bring the chariot up short and step out.

Sitting above the contestants was a powerfully-built, muscular man. His dark hair flowed in curls over his shoulders, and his smile was radiant, confident. His white robe was trimmed with gold and diamonds, and was open at the chest. He laughed and ate as the athletes before him competed for his applause, which he gave generously and often between large gulps of purple wine and nectar.

The awesome figure was surrounded by women of every stripe—white, black, yellow—and nymphs and other creatures as well. They fawned over him, laughing when he spoke, feeding him strawberries and pieces of roast. He would often reach out, take one in the curve of his arm, and embrace her.

That must be Zeus. Daphne shook her head, torn between admiration and disgust. *Only he would be groping that many asses at once.*

From behind her, a shrill note sounded. The call resonated throughout Olympus, heard by all. Zeus stirred from his seat, his countenance turning from joy to concern in less than a second. The competitions and revelry ceased, and everyone was quiet.

"Oh my God." Daphne turned toward the gate. "It...no. Please, no."

At the end of the thoroughfare were twenty men and women in much older versions of the uniform Chloe and her companions had worn—white robes with red crosses emblazoned on the front. They all carried weapons, swords and knives and axes, and their shields bore the same emblem as their chests. The gatekeeper had already been torn apart, sliced in a dozen places with his flute still in his mouth.

Blood pooled in the streets.

I don't want to see this. Daphne began to retreat, her head turning one way, then the other, searching for shelter or escape. *I don't want to watch them die.*

"Halt!" A man, radiating authority and arrogance, stepped through the crowd and in front of the group of twenty. He wore bronze armor and, at his side, a wicked sword, serrated edges ruddy, as if dripping blood. "You –"

One of the Crusaders flicked his hand forward, and a dagger flew out, landing in the soft throat of the speaker. He gurgled, his hand fumbling at the weapon embedded in his flesh, then fell.

Apollo's voice seemed to ring in Daphne's mind. *My half-brother Ares was first to fall. He stood before the invaders with his blade dripping blood, and he bellowed his challenge.*

After a moment of silence, the crowd of immortals, demigods, and spirits began to scream, a stampede in the making, pushing and shoving at each other in an attempt to escape. The Crusaders moved with a purpose, marching through the streets, their leader giving orders with hand gestures and concise commands. Small groups broke off from the main pack, kicking down the doors of Olympian houses and buildings, shouts of terror erupting from within wherever they went.

Four giants with one eye, Cyclopes, could be seen on a side-street, hammering at the ground with their great clubs and mallets. Daphne could not see their enemies, but she watched, her hand over her mouth, as each Cyclops was felled, the impact of their bodies shaking the mountaintop when they landed.

When the last was down, Daphne heard the clanging of metal, then an outcry, cut short.

Hephaestus was next.

Great Zeus strode out of the amphitheater, his muscles bunching under his robe. Electricity had begun to crackle around him, and his face was anger incarnate. When he stepped into the road and saw the invaders, he gave voice to a tremendous bellow. The force of the cry knocked Daphne off of her feet.

In response to his call, the sky around Olympus darkened with thunderclouds. Lightning flashed amongst them, and the *booming* sounds resembled artillery fired in the distance. He extended his hand and the heavens answered his call, javelins of light lancing from the clouds into the group of Crusaders. The first bolt killed three, searing burns visible through their charred uniforms, and there was a cheer from the nearby onlookers.

The remaining attackers formed up, blades advanced, passing by the alleyway Daphne was huddled in as she observed the massacre. From this distance, she could see the symbols forged in the blades. *Those must be the holy runes that Apollo was talking about. What's letting them kill the gods.*

Zeus threw himself at the formation, and his strength was evident—he picked up a Crusader in each hand and threw them in an arc which took them off the mountaintop, screaming the whole way down. He grabbed another's head in his hands and crushed it, blood, brains, and bone running between his fingers.

Behind Zeus, more gods were coming to join the battle. Daphne could see proud Athena, wielding the great shield Aegis, and wild Artemis with her silver bow, looking so much like her brother. Hermes flew from the palace, trumpeting the rallying cry, and a dozen minor deities responded.

How do they lose? Despite herself, Daphne leaned in closer to the battle. *There's so many of them. Even if some die...*

Daphne blinked, and the world shattered.

A wide-bladed sword shoved its way through Zeus' chest, covered in dripping blood. The king of the gods faltered, his mouth coming unhinged, his hands grasping the blade. His eyes rolled back in his head, and, mirroring his fall, the thunderheads dispersed, scattering with the four winds. All of Olympus seemed to darken, and the cheering creatures gasped in horror.

As Zeus' body hit the ground, Daphne watched to see who was behind him, holding the sword. A black-haired beauty with crazed red eyes, dressed in a gown which, on the surface, resembled that of the other Olympians, but was a mishmash of patterns and fabrics. Instead of sandals, she wore bronze boots, and underneath her robe was armor from hundreds of years ago, patched together from all over the world.

But none of this drew Daphne's attention so much as the madness in her smile. Her teeth were white, but out of place, like someone in desperate need of braces. She seemed constantly on the edge of laughter, even as she pulled the blade from Zeus and held it aloft.

A glowing sphere, crackling lightning, rolled away from his hand. His attacker knelt down and took it up, the light shining in her face as if she held a flashlight beneath it.

The onrushing tide of divinities faltered. Athena looked back and forth from her fallen father to his murderer, her spear falling to her side, held loosely in her grip.

"...Eris?" The named goddess turned to face her cousins. "Why have...why have you done this?"

Eris buckled over, her chest heaving with raucous, discordant laughter. The remaining Crusaders marched onward, weapons leveled at the rest of the gods. "Why not, my sister?" She shook her head, still laughing, as she lifted the glowing orb that she had taken from Zeus. "Family is always such a burden."

With a magnificent *ka-thoom*, a great bolt of lightning leapt from the ball at the clustered immortals. Athena raised the Aegis, but those beside her had no such defense and were struck down as the lightning split into a myriad of smaller strikes, each with its own target. Sparks flew off the surface of the great shield, ricocheting in all directions and dazzling Daphne with their brightness; she retreated behind the corner of the building to regain her vision and bearings.

From her shelter, she heard the *ka-thoom, ka-thoom* as Eris took aim at others with Zeus' mighty thunderbolt. She heard the screams of those under attack silenced in the aftermath of the heavenly artillery strikes, and could smell the ozone, thick and metallic in the air.

At last, the blasts stopped, and Daphne could no longer feel the shuddering in the ground beneath her. She peeked around the corner again to survey the situation.

Athena. She's still alive.

The Goddess of Wisdom held the Aegis before her, smoking but unscathed. Her spear was clasped in the other hand and raised in a defensive stance. Eris lowered the thunderbolt and laughed as the Crusaders surrounded her cousin.

"Apollo was wrong. It was not the power of some other god that was our undoing." Athena loosened her grasp on her weapon. "It was one of our own."

"Dearest Athena, *that* was your mistake." She raised the hand that held the orb. "You actually believed that you were part of something, a piece of a whole, instead of one being amongst many." She brought the hand down. "Your wisdom failed you, sister."

As one, the surrounding Crusaders launched themselves at the goddess. Athena did not swing her spear, did not raise the Aegis. Her grey eyes turned to the side, her face resigned, as death approached her.

"No!" Daphne cried out, breaking her cover and running toward the battle. "You can't!"

No one seemed to hear her; Eris' laughter continued, and bright red blood flew into the air, a perverse shower that rained up before coming down again. Daphne lost track of Athena in the melee, and by the time she reached the battlefield, it was over. The goddess' eyes were closed, her body rent in dozens of places.

"Stay here and wait for the rest." Eris turned her back on the Crusaders. "They will be here soon." She stopped, turned her head back, gave a half-smile. "Remember, God wills it!"

"*God wills it!*" The commander of the unit began barking orders, separating his surviving men into groups. As they scattered to and fro, Daphne crept closer to Athena's body.

The violence visited upon her had left her face untouched. She had a gentle beauty, but even so Daphne could see the lines of wisdom etched in the goddess' brow. She extended a hand to brush the hair from Athena's face, glancing over at where Eris stood as she did so.

Her motions froze, and she gasped.

Eris was walking to the bodies of the immortals the Crusaders had defeated. She would stand over them, touch their foreheads, and the corpses would vanish in a shower of red and purple light followed by a small *pop*. In the pulses of light, Eris' face was hideous, almost a clown's mask of grinning terror, fiendish pleasure stamped over her every feature.

Daphne shuddered, turning back to Athena's dead body.

The grey eyes were staring at her.

She backpedaled on her hands and feet several steps, her heart moving into the beat of a drum solo.

"We don't have much time." The goddess' voice was a whisper now, husky, on the verge of breaking. "Come here, Daphne. Please."

Daphne crept forward again. "Wh-what can I do?"

The corners of Athena's mouth twitched. "Everything. Listen."

Daphne listened.

Chapter Twenty

"Hello, Apollo."

The Sun God's eyes opened at the sound of the woman's voice. Chloe was standing above him, her face inverted over his as he lay on the steel bed, bindings tight.

"You again." Apollo made a brief effort of trying to break free from his chains, but it was obvious that he could not. "I have nothing to say to you."

"Of course you don't." Chloe began to walk around him, forcing him to follow her with his eyes. "You know, you've led us on quite the chase, my friend. It's been very difficult tracking you down over these centuries."

Apollo stilled his struggle, but did not reply.

"Still, I suppose it was inevitable. I mean, you never could keep it in your pants, could you?" Chloe began to laugh, speaking through the breaks in hilarity. "I mean, you and your father, am I right? And Poseidon, too, just…" She broke down, holding on to a nearby computer desk for support. "If it had two legs, wasn't missing too many teeth, and had somewhere for you to put it, you didn't hold back!"

Despite the imminent danger he was in, Apollo spoke up. "How dare you speak of my family that way? You, heiress to their murders. They lie on your head just as much as on your predecessors!"

"More, perhaps." Chloe pushed herself back to a full stand. "But don't worry about that. You and I are about to have some special time together, Shining One."

"You can do nothing to me, woman." Apollo turned his eyes to the ceiling, away from his captor. "My love is beyond your reach, and my family is dead. I welcome oblivion."

"See, that's your mistake." Chloe trailed her fingers across Apollo's well-muscled arm before stopping at his wrist. "You always were such an optimist."

Apollo's head snapped toward her. In the fluorescents, Chloe's eyes seemed to glow red, and her smile was wide, her teeth like a bear trap. She held a large syringe in one hand.

"Whoever said that you were going to get to *die* after all this?"

~~~

The burning chariot descended to Earth, its flames damping as it landed. Daphne adjusted the band on her wrist that she had received from Athena, emblazoned with the snarling head of a woman with snakes for hair—a Gorgon.

"Good boys." She rubbed the horses' noses, and they nickered and pressed their heads against her hands. "Stay here, okay? I should be back in a few minutes."

Daphne turned away from the chariot and took in her surroundings. The mountainside was dry and sheer, but a myriad of small cracks ran across the rock face she approached. Tiny creeper vines dug their shoots into these cracks, searching for sustenance.

"Now, if I were a secret entrance..." Daphne ran her fingers along the network of ridges and crevices in the rock. "Damn it!" She pulled her hands away, a bloody cut across the pad of one finger. She stuck it in her mouth, and looked up the cliff. "I don't suppose that a password or anything would work, like in Lord of the Rings, huh?"

No answer.

"Of course not. Okay." Daphne walked a few paces away from the rock, then turned back around and sat down, still nursing her wounded finger. She looked up as a jet streaked across the sky, shook her
~~~

head, then began looking for something to write with. She grabbed a small, fallen stick and began to write in the dirt.

Garden of Hera. Guarded by Ladon and Hesperides. She took her finger out of her mouth and grabbed part of her sleeve that had been torn by her leap through the window. A brief tug and a short tearing sound later, she had a makeshift bandage, which she wrapped around her injury to stem the bleeding before continuing her brainstorm.

"Right then." *Atlas. Heracles. Eris.* She pursed her lips. *Kallisti.*

"The apple that started the Trojan War. Bitch." She sat back on her haunches. "So how do I get in? Atlas got in because the keepers were his daughters. Eris...was a goddess. Who knows how she did it?" She rubbed her temples. "Damn it, Athena! I know you were dying and all, but couldn't you have told me how the hell to get in here?"

Go to the Garden, where the golden apples are grown for Hera. His horses know the way. Athena's voice was strong and clear in her memory. *You are our last hope.*

"The golden apples are grown for Hera." Daphne stood up. *Is it really that simple?* She walked once more to the mountainside and placed her hands against the rock.

"In Hera's name, open the way to the Garden. The Queen of the Gods commands it."

She waited, her heartbeats loud in her ears. A gust of wind kicked up, stirring sand and dirt, causing her to close her eyes against the grit.

She opened them again.

Nothing had changed.

"Damn it!" She kicked at the unyielding stone, which did nothing except give her pain in her foot to match that in her finger. She lost her balance and fell back on the ground.

"It does no good to kick stone, little dryad. Better to go around it than through."

"Thanks for the tip." Daphne held her head in her hands. "Doesn't help me right –"

Wait, what?

Daphne picked her head back up, and, like an owl, turned it round until she saw who was speaking.

Behind her, stretching up twenty feet over her head and staring down at her with black, shining eyes, was a giant serpent. It was so wide that she couldn't have wrapped her arms around it, and its tongue was golden, flicking in and out of its mouth as it tasted the air.

Daphne's first reaction was nigh-instantaneous panic, but she fought it down. "...Who are you?" She stood. "I hope you aren't planning on eating me."

The snake laughed, a machine gun of hissing sounds. "That depends on why you invoke the Mother Goddess's name, little dryad." He twisted into a coil, bringing his head down to a height of ten feet or so.

"As for who I am...I am Ladon, Guardian of the Garden." He bobbed his head in a semblance of a bow, then moved his sinuous coils to allow the woman to see what lay beyond—a once-glorious orchard filled with fruit trees. They stretched dozens, hundreds, of feet into the air, but were now choked by the growth of weeds and vines. Ladon's tail end reached up from the ground into one of the great trees, disappearing amongst the foliage. "If you seek my companions, they are gone. When the gods fell, they abandoned their station, and ran to their deaths." A moment of silence. "Now...who are you? I have not heard anyone invoke the Goddess in some time, you see." The snake's head moved forward, hovering over Daphne.

"I..." She shook her head and swallowed down her fear. "I am Daphne. I come on behalf of all the Olympians. They –"

Ladon reared back, his fangs extending from its mouth. "The Olympians are slain! All of them are dead! You shall die for your falsehoods!!"

"No!" Daphne raised her hands to defend herself. "Apollo still lives! He –"

Ladon lunged forward, Venom dripped from its mouth as he sped toward Daphne, who stepped back in horror.

As the snake was about to sink his teeth into her flesh, there was a bright flash of light and the sound of something large striking metal. Daphne's armband, given to her by Athena, had transformed into the shield Aegis, the impenetrable bulwark. Ladon's head recoiled from the impact, and he screamed, turning away and hiding his eyes from the metal which had begun to pulse with power on Daphne's arm.

"Put it away!" Ladon's coils undulated, moving over each other with a whispery, papery sound. "I will not strike again! Put it away!"

Daphne relaxed her shoulders, but kept the shield up. "What assurances do I have? How do I know you won't just attack me as soon as I put this down?"

"I cannot act against an emissary of the gods! That shield belongs to Lord Zeus himself." The serpent's head peeked up, then retreated again. "Name your commands, and I will serve!"

Daphne nodded. *Okay. Here goes.* She closed her eyes, and thought at the shield. *Away, until I need you.*

One more bright flash, and the shield had reverted to the armband. "Very well, Ladon. It is gone."

Ladon peeked once again, then slithered toward Daphne. This time, his head stayed low to the ground, and he kept a respectful distance. "I serve you, mistress. What do you demand of Ladon?"

Daphne licked her lips. "Athena left something here, long ago. She said that it could help me save Apollo now. Do you know what it was?"

Ladon bobbed his head again. "The relics that Perseus wielded when he slew the Gorgon whose head adorns the shield you bear." He turned and climbed up a nearby tree. "I have guarded them for thousands of yearsss." A large burlap sack landed on the ground, and Ladon followed it down the trunk. "They are yours."

Daphne crept over to the bag, keeping a wary eye on the giant snake watching her, then opened it. Within were three things—a pair of sandals with wings on the side, a bronze helmet with nose guard and a Mohawk, and a sword, gleaming silver and curved, almost like a sickle or scythe. She hefted the blade.

"This is so light." She spun it in her hand, and it seemed to respond to her desires as it moved, remaining in her grasp despite her lack of training with the weapon.

"The Harpe." Ladon's voice was reverent, awed. "First wielded by Cronos, then by Perseus. Now by you. The sandals belonged to Hermes, and the helmet to Hades."

Daphne brought out the helm. "You mean...this is the Helmet of Invisibility? Like, it'll make me invisible? Really?"

Ladon nodded his head. "Together, these relics make you the equal of almost any god." His tongue flicked out twice, thrice. "...Apollo lives?"

Daphne paused in her admiration of the items and bowed her head. "Yeah, but I don't know how long." She stood, closing the bag, and took a breath. "I need to get moving."

Ladon turned away from her again, slithering toward the center of the garden. Daphne followed, squinting her eyes to keep track of him. She watched as the snake climbed another tree—this one was massive, stretching a football field across at the crown. Its leaves seemed to shine like gold, radiating the light of the sun back toward the heavens.

When he returned, there was a small golden fruit between his lips. He placed the fruit on the ground before speaking.

"This fruit is the reason great Hera set me to watch the Garden. This is the Apple of Immortality. If Apollo is wounded or dying—perhaps even dead—this will restore him."

Daphne picked it up. It was not an apple, exactly—it had more bumps and was oblong—but its skin was metallic gold, and it was heavy.

"Take it with you." Ladon sighed and settled to the ground. "Now, I can finally rest."

Daphne furrowed her brow and leaned closer to the snake. "What do you mean?"

He stirred and nodded toward the fruit. "Hera asked me to guard the Apple of Immortality. Now that I have given it away, the gift she gave me will falter, and I will die." A large breath exited his nostrils. "At last."

His eyes closed.

Tears began to sting Daphne's eyes. She laid a hand on Ladon's head. "Then sleep, great Guardian, and know that you did your job well. You were saving this apple for this day. Your mission is fulfilled."

Ladon opened one eye. "And you, Dryad. I can see the signs of two births upon you. Perhaps this one was so that you could save the Sun God as well." His eye closed again. "Perhaps this is why we were both born."

The snake's gigantic body shuddered, and then, before Daphne's eyes, it began to decompose. Mushrooms and mold crept over the body as she stared, eating away the flesh. Huge chunks of meat dropped off and rotted on the ground, and, within seconds, all that was left was the enormous skeleton of the ancient serpent.

Daphne bowed her head, then stood. Around her, the entire garden was following suit, following its last guardian into death. The trees turned yellow, then brown, their leaves falling toward the ground and disintegrating into nothing before touching down. From Ladon's last resting place, a circle of decay radiated outward, the grass crumbling into dust and dirt. A minute later, nothing save Daphne was left alive in the great Garden of the Hesperides.

Well, nothing except me and this fruit. Daphne hefted the Apple, then put into the bag along with the relics. *All right. It's time.*

Excerpt from Cassandra's Diary—Sept 5th

The Laughing Woman hides behind a mask, but the mask wears thin. She will cast it off soon, and her vengeance will be complete. The world will splinter into ten thousand fragments, and she will keep each one close that it can never connect to another.

The Golden Man cries out, his lips holding back the sound that his heart makes. She uses him, a conduit to her greater desires. She violates him in every way—body, spirit, soul—and enjoys every moment.

She has given herself over to what she is, rather than what she could be. She has learned the worst parts of being human.

The Twice-Born races toward her in a comet, a burning star. Hope burns brighter in her heart than in that star, but...

And that's it. The vision stopped there. What does it mean? I've never seen things like this before. Who are these people? And what are they doing?

Well, I know one thing. It'll be nice to be at college again, even if most of the people there avoid me like the plague. My parents still tiptoe around me, like I'm going to curse them by looking at them or something.

My taxi is here. Off I go!

Chapter Twenty-One

Daphne slipped off the sandals and tossed the bag into the chariot. "You know, flying with these takes a little getting used to."

The nearest stallion shook its head and whinnied.

"Yeah, I know that flying is old hat to you two." She slipped into her seat and flicked the reins; the horses turned round and began their takeoff run. "But I'm accustomed to being land-bound."

Once more, the chariot rose up into the sky. Daphne palmed the golden fruit, turning it one way, than another. Its skin shimmered in the sunlight, and she could find no blemishes on it.

The Apple of Immortality. She inhaled; her nose was met by the luscious smell of baked apples and cinnamon. *What if...*

She opened her eyes. Her hand had brought the fruit to within an inch of her mouth, and her lips had parted and teeth had bared. She shook her head and threw the fruit into the bag as well.

"No, thank you." A shudder ran through her, and she turned herself away from where the fruit lay. "Okay, now, last things last. Where's that damn owl?"

Daphne craned her neck, looking up at the cliffs, in the sparse foliage, in the few trees. There were no owls to be found.

She closed her eyes again and took a deep breath. "All right. Athena isn't a bitch. She's not trying to mess with me or be deliberately vague, but she wants me to think. Goddess of Wisdom. Okay." She opened her eyes. "There's no owl because it's too obvious. They might notice a god-sent owl leading a chariot of fire. Okay. So, instead..."

Perched on the leading edge, like the figurehead of a ship, was a tiny white owl figurine. Its claws were wrapped around an olive branch. Its head bobbed up and down on a small spring.

"A bobble-head?" Daphne leaned over and plucked the figurine from its perch. "Seriously?"

As she turned the trinket in her hand to examine it, the owl's head swiveled. It continued pointing in the same direction, regardless of which way she moved.

"All right, then." Her right hand snaked out and tugged upward on the reins, bringing the horses higher in the sky. "Here I come, Chloe."

~~~

Chloe's fingernails dug into her palm, and red blood spattered on the floor. The terrified naiad glanced down at the sound of the droplets, then back up at the Crusader's angry eyes.

"I...I'm sorry. She got away. I had her, but I didn't expect –"

"Shut up." Chloe brought her bleeding hand up to her mouth, closed in a fist. "You had one job. One simple thing that I needed you to do." She spun, advancing on the water nymph, grabbing her by her shirt. "You have proven yourself worthless as a tool."

Climethea's eyes were wide, terrified. "Please, I'm sorry. Don't kill me."

"Oh, I won't." That wicked, scythe-like smile reemerged. "And I won't kill him, either." She dropped her companion to the ground and reached behind her nearby chair. "But you might wish I had."

Climethea picked herself off the ground. "What do you–"

Her words died as she stared down the haft of the lead arrow pointed in her face. Chloe's eyes glowed red, the glow lighting up her cheeks and forehead behind the bow.
~~~

"Too bad for you." The arrow fired and sank into the naiad's chest, rippling and vanishing as it entered. Climethea watched as it drove through her body, then looked back up at Chloe. Tears filled her eyes.

"Why?"

"Because you dared." Chloe sat back in her chair, dropping the weapon beside it. "You dared think that you could be part of something bigger, that he could love you and you him."

"But, but I –"

"Hate him now. Despise him. The thought of him makes you nauseous." Chloe leaned in, resting her chin on her fingertips. "Now imagine his hand caressing your skin, trailing down from the nape of your neck to your –"

"No!" Climethea shook her head, curling in on herself like a child watching a horror film. "Stop!"

Chloe waved her hand. "Go away. Suffer your fate somewhere else, if you will. I have no further time for you."

Climethea tried to speak, but a large-bodied Crusader came around the corner and took her by her shoulders, escorting her, weeping, out of the room.

"Jorge." Another man, young, dark-skinned, stepped in. "Bring me the Eye, if you would."

"Yes, Commander." The man bowed, holding his hand to his chest as he left the room.

~~~

"Again, seriously?" Daphne peeked over the edge of the chariot again at the ground below. "They're down there?"

Underneath, the surface of the ocean was churning, blades of water swirling around a great whirlpool. Easily five miles across, it stretched almost as far as Daphne could see.

A cruise liner moseyed through the water, towing a hang glider, heading straight for the vortex. As Daphne watched, it dipped down, its bow edging out over the empty space below before tipping over and sliding down the edge.

"Shit! Those people!" Daphne began rushing to tug her winged sandals on. She looked down as she struggled to slip the straps over her heels.

"What the hell?"

The passengers of the ship seemed unaware that anything was happening. They carried on drinking their martinis, sunning themselves on the deck, and playing shuffleboard even as the ship turned vertical and descended into the depths of the whirlpool. They paid no mind to the spray that showered around them, nor to the swirling rapids and the deafening roar that came from them.
~~~

She kept watching. *Someone has to notice. I mean, they just went down like five hundred feet.* But no one did.

She shook her head. *I wonder what kind of things I've been missing my whole life, if there can be monster whirlpools in the middle of the ocean that no one sees.*

The chariot dipped as it circled around the vortex, and Daphne struggled to remember what she had heard about this whirlpool.

"It was supposed to be a monster that ate sailors." She grimaced. "I *really* hope that, like, Percy Jackson killed this thing already, or that it decided to move on to better feeding grounds, or something."

The horses tossed their heads, keeping the chariot just out of reach of the splashing water.

"Okay, boys." Daphne tightened the last strap on her sandals. "Go for it."

As one, the stallions rose up into the air, then flipped end over end, nose-diving into the swirling maelstrom of watery death. As they descended toward the point of the vortex, Daphne closed her eyes and picked the owl up off the dash.

Five seconds. I really hope that this isn't a mistake.

Four.

Three.

Two.

One.

...

She opened her eyes. There was no more maelstrom, no more raging water or cruise liner. The chariot was, once again, flying through the air, and the sun shone down on the ground. The landscape was criss-crossed with rivers, and trees climbed the slope of a nearby mountain.

Except...everything was wrong.

Black seagulls tore at each other, scattering droplets of blood throughout the air as several of them plummeted from the sky. On the ground, a gang of rabbits surrounded a grey wolf and dug into it, teeth severing sinew and bone and leaving the predator bleeding from a dozen places before it died. Once it was down, the rabbits ran off, looking for their next target.

Even the trees. The oaks, pines, and chestnut trees were engaged in a war. Branches fought one another—Daphne could see them growing and shifting before her eyes—each struggling to climb higher than the other to claim precious sunlight for itself. Other vines and creepers stretched out to entwine and entangle, bending and breaking branches on a slow-motion battlefield.

It's like... Daphne stared over the landscape. *Everything is trying to kill everything else. It's insane.* Something in the distance caught her eye.

Olympus. Of course.

In this dark reflection of Earth, Olympus still stood tall and proud, although it appeared sharper, its slopes less forgiving. Instead of rainclouds surrounding the mountaintop and obscuring it from view, however, there was a red mist, like a fog of blood. Instead of thunderclaps echoing from within, there were screams and sounds of combat.

The perfect place for Discord. Daphne looked down at the owl figurine she still held in her hand. Its beak was pointed straight at the cloud.

"You know what to do." She pointed toward the red mist. "He's in there."

~~~

The Stygian Eye hovered in the middle of the room. The lights were off and the windows closed, and the only light visible radiated from the orb in the center.

"Show me."

The glowing sphere expanded until it took up a quarter of the room. Colors flickered within, resolving into a picture of the chariot, flames streaking from its sides as it bore down on the Headquarters of the Crusaders. Hawks and gulls swept around it, diving at the burning missile in an ill-fated attempt to do battle, only to turn into matchsticks and paper in the fire.
~~~

Chloe cocked her head. "What the hell is she doing?"

The chariot continued to approach. It showed no sign of slowing down; instead, it angled downward as it passed through the crimson clouds. The stallions pulling the vehicle were snorting smoke and sweating flame, running like thoroughbreds pushed to the finish line.

"No." Chloe watched a moment longer, then laughed. "I guess I was wrong about you, little girl. Good to see you have some grit to you after all." She reached down to her belt and pulled out her hand-held radio.

"We have incoming. Fire the AA missiles."

A few seconds later, the building trembled and four smoke-trails were lancing through the sky toward the invading chariot. The horses broke off their charge, swinging upward in a curving arc like a roller-coaster, the missiles spiraling as they followed behind. Up and down, side to side they went, slipping in and around the missiles' paths.

"Do we have any more missiles?" Chloe frowned. "Those ones are about to run out of fucking gas."

"Yes, Commander."

"Then fire all of them. I want that chariot brought down *now*."

"At once, Commander."

Eight more projectiles fired toward Apollo's chariot, and the stallions seemed to panic for a moment, abandoning their aerial acrobatics in favor of an all-out retreat. They turned tail and ran, their cargo bouncing behind them before steadying in their path.

"Not too clever after all, then. It's too bad –" Chloe cut off her own sentence, staring at the scrying window. "Freeze image!"

Like she had hit pause on a DVD player, the moving figures stopped in their tracks, still and silent. She moved toward the pictured scene, and the flow of blood from her cut palm renewed as her nails dug in once again.

"Zoom in on the chariot."

The back of the chariot expanded to ten times its original size. The Eye brought it forward in clear detail.

"Fucking bitch!" Chloe turned and stormed out of the room, barking orders on her radio between expletives. The door slammed, and the image remained, frozen in the middle of the room.

Daphne was not in the chariot.

Chapter Twenty-Two

Guess they figured it out. The blare of alarms and the running of troops echoed through the many hallways, a cacophonous medley of controlled fear. Daphne kept herself low, clutching the sickle-sword Harpe in one hand and the bobble-head owl in the other. The Aegis was strapped to her left arm.

Harry Potter's got nothing on this helmet, though, I'll tell you that. A group of guards turned the corner in front of Daphne, causing her to crush herself against the wall to avoid an accidental collision. Despite the fact that the movement caused her headgear to bang against the building, none of them gave her a second glance, running by as they checked their ammo and locked and loaded their rifles and pistols. *It's hard when you can't even see yourself, though.* A suppressed laugh and a brief check to make sure no one had heard her, then she was moving again.

Take it slow, Daph, take it slow. She continued creeping forward, pausing at each intersection to check her direction, suppressing the urge to sprint down the hallway, screaming the sun god's name. *While they're looking for you, they aren't killing him. If you get caught, you won't be doing him any good.*

A contingent of Crusaders was camped out in the four-direction crossroads ahead, scanning each hallway with their rifles. A call came over their radios.

"This is Team Seven, go ahead."

"Team Seven, this is Dis. Switch to infrared. We're going dark."

Oh, crap. Does the helmet hide me from infrared?

"Roger that, Dis. Going dark. Seven out." The team members nodded to each other, rooting through their equipment, two at a time, to extract pairs of high-tech goggles and secure them over their eyes.

Daphne kept moving closer, lowering herself into a crawl. The Aegis scraped along the ground, but the sound was muted by the power of Hades' Helm. The guards finished putting on their goggles just as she finished crossing their position and had returned to a walking position.

The radio hissed again.

"Okay, Dis. This is Seven. We're go for dark."

"Copy that, Seven. Going dark."

The lights shut down. There was no illumination, not even safety lights or strips along the floor. There were also no nearby windows, so the hallways were black, filled with inky darkness. A soft *click* and the guards' goggles were active, picking up heat patterns in the absence of visible light.

The Helm of Darkness began to shed a soft blue light, illuminating Daphne's surroundings. Despite being lit up like a field at moonrise, the guards gave no indication that they could see anything amiss.

Sweet. It's like a ghost light or something.

Daphne turned the corner and put her back against the wall.

"Hey, did you guys see that?"

"What?"

"I thought I saw something disappear around that corner."

Footsteps sounded, coming down the hall toward her. *At least these guys have read the Evil Overlord List. No bad movie mistakes for them.* Daphne smiled in spite of herself.

Two guards came round the corner, scanning the area in front of them, rifles at the ready. Several seconds went by.

"I don't see anything, Phil."

"Guess not. We would have heard if someone went running down that way."

Another few moments. "You sure you saw something? If you did, we should call it in anyway."

Phil shook his head. "I wasn't sure. It was just a blink, out of the corner of my eye, you know? Could've easily just been the image resolving."

His companion tapped his foot. "The Commander would be pissed if we let that girl get by us, you know?"

A chuckle. "Sure, but, what? She's invisible or something? We didn't see her go by, and she's totally in the dark. I don't think it'll be long before someone finds her."

Phil's friend relaxed his stance. "Yeah. Guess I'm just a little jumpy. Let's get back, okay?"

"Yeah."

The two turned around and ran to meet up with the others. Daphne released the breath she hadn't realized she was holding.

Okay. She floated down from her position on the ceiling, still clutching blade and bird in her hands. *Where are you, Apollo?*

The guards had taken up their positions around the possible entrances to the compound, so Daphne encountered very few as she made her way through to the center. Most of the rooms were empty, barren except for a little bit of furniture—a chair, a bookshelf, a sparring dummy.

What do these guys do here all day? Daphne ducked through yet another suite of rooms, following the owl's direction as best she could. *No TV, no beds. It's almost like –*

She brought herself up short as she entered the next room. Unlike the others, this one was decked out as a medical patient's room. There was a bed surrounded by a curtain, and the entire area smelled of bleach and antiseptics. A gentle *beep, beep* coming from the equipment near the bed told Daphne that there was someone on it, and that the someone was alive.

She glanced down at the bird again. Its beak indicated a right turn.

Daphne began to move past the bed toward the door, but she heard a ragged breath from the person behind the curtains and her head turned to look. Hanging out from the bed was a slight, delicate hand.

The fingernails of that hand were a deep, royal blue.

A memory flashed in Daphne's mind of those same fingernails atop her own hand as the owner spoke comfort...and madness.

"Cassie!" Daphne reached out and pulled back the curtain, almost tearing it from its moorings. Under the thin, sterile hospital sheets lay the battered, beaten form of her friend. An IV was in her arm, dripping clear liquid through a tube into her bloodstream, and electrodes were attached to her chest and head.

"No." Tears dripped on the floor, and the Harpe and owl tumbled to the ground.

Cassandra's eye sockets were covered by white bandages, red stains visible at the edge of the wrappings. Daphne reached out and took her friend's hand in both of hers. "Cassie? Cassie, are you awake? Can you hear me?"

There was no answer. Daphne's head bowed as she cried over her friend. "I'm so sorry, Cassie. I didn't know. I couldn't know. I had this dream about you, but Apollo said that it wasn't a prophecy, so I –"

"He was Apollo?"

Daphne's head whipped around to look into the face of the other girl. "Hey."

Cassandra's dry, cracked lips moved. "That's for horses, Daphne." She shuddered, took a deep breath. "What's going on? Why can't I see?" Her hands fumbled, uncoordinated movements reaching for her face. Daphne took hold of her hands again and brought them back down.

"Cassie...they..." Daphne's voice broke. "They...they took your eyes."

Cassandra froze; her muscles tensed, and she pulled her hands away from Daphne's grip and her fingertips ran over the rough bandages. Her lip began to shake and her chest to hitch as deep, sobbing gasps forced their way out.

Daphne knelt by her friend's bedside, unable to speak. Long minutes went by; Crusaders ran by the room as they searched the complex for the intruder, but Daphne couldn't bring herself to move away.

Finally, Cassandra's weeping began to subside. She reached out toward Daphne again, and the young woman grabbed the flailing hands and held them close.

"I shouldn't complain." A thin, weak laugh escaped her, coupled with a sad smile. "At least now I won't have to see people looking at me funny, huh?"

Daphne kissed her friend on the forehead. "I'm so sorry, Cassie. It...it's all my fault. I shouldn't have left with him, I should have been there –"

"Bullshit, Daph." Cassandra used one hand to pull out the needle of the IV from her other arm. "If the God of the Sun had asked me to go with him, you can bet I'd have done the exact same thing."

"But –"

"Anyway, what's going on?" Cassandra started pawing at the sheets, the bedframe. "Where am I?"

"You're...the Crusaders captured you." Daphne leaned in closer as another group of voices went by. "I think they must have used your...used you to trap Apollo."

Cassandra stopped her explorations and whipped her head back around to Daphne. "They trapped him? But...but..."

Daphne reached up to smooth Cassandra's hair and calm her. "I know. I'm going to get him out of here." She tilted her head and smiled. "Don't worry. I've got help."

Cassandra laid back and returned Daphne's unseen smile. "Good. You'll make it. You'll save him."

Daphne nodded, then slipped her hands under her friend. "First, we're going to get you out of here."

The injured woman's hands locked onto the metal frame of the bed. "Like hell you are!"

Daphne recoiled from the power and sharpness of Cassandra's voice. "What?"

"Look. This sucks, but there's nothing you can do about it right now." Cassandra did her best to draw herself into a half-sitting position. "But if Apollo dies, or whatever it is they're going to do to him...then that's it. He is the Golden Man, and is the last one standing between this world and eternal strife."

"Cassie." Daphne returned to her position by the bed. "I can't just leave you here."

"Yes. You can, and you will. If you don't, there will be guards coming by in about two minutes, so pick up that shit and get out of here." She motioned with her head to the doorway.

Daphne hesitated for a moment, then nodded. "All right. I'll be back for you, Cassie."

Cassandra's stern look faded, and she touched her friend's hand again. "I know you will." As Daphne moved away from the bed, Cassandra gasped.

"What is it?"

Cassandra's face was blank, like it had been at the diner when she recounted her vision of her grandmother's death. "The soldiers train their guns down the hallway. The metal shines in the light—the only light for miles, it seems. They see someone, and they cannot shoot."

Daphne shook her head. "I don't understand."

"Daphne." Cassandra's face had returned to normal. "If the soldiers don't see you, you will not succeed. You cannot stay hidden from them."

"What? That doesn't –"

"Daphne, you need to go. Trust me. Please."

Daphne scooped up the owl figurine and the golden sickle sword, nodded. "I do." She hustled out of the room, and Cassandra's eyeless face followed her on her way out.

"Thank you, Daphne. I'll miss you." She started struggling to get out of the bed. "But there's something that you need me to do."

~~~

Chloe stood in the command center, listening to the reports coming in from the Crusaders. No sign of Daphne or of anyone else.

Rivulets of blood flowed down both palms and her fingers, pit-patting on the ground as she paced around the room.
~~~

"The Eye can't find her." Several of the nearby guards were watching her as she moved, like a caged animal that was so eager to hunt that its keepers were afraid of it. "So she's either dead, or she has her own magic. But we have it all. There's nothing left, we made sure."

"...Commander?" One of the Crusaders stepped forward, hand raised. Chloe stopped in her tracks, turning on the balls of her feet to look at the young man.

He swallowed.

"...Yes?" Her eyes were smoldering red now, and she took a step toward him. "Do you have something to say?"

"Well...I was thinking that, if she's here looking for *him*, then maybe we could just wait for her there?" When Chloe's countenance did not change, the Crusader stepped back, his head bowed, waiting for death.

Seconds passed. Chloe turned away, and her fury seemed to subside. She pursed her lips and turned her head back toward the Crusaders.

"...You're right." The tension in the room vanished, and the speaking Crusader took a deep breath before getting on his radio.

"Teams two, five, six, and eight, converge on the main project room. Do not let anyone in. I say again..."

Chloe motioned for the people in the room to leave, shooing them out with her hands. She followed behind, closing the door as she left.

~~~

Holy hell. Daphne took another peek around the corner. *Did they call in the National Guard or something?*

The door that her supernatural compass was pointing to had been locked down *hard*. At least four separate groups of commandos were set up, staggered across the hall so as not to get in each other's way. Firearms of every stripe were aimed downrange, and the barrel openings called her, challenged her, terrified her.

Get it together, Daphne. She hoisted the Aegis, and the ancient metal seemed to radiate warmth, banishing the chill of fear from her body and heart. *Time to go. God, I hope you're right about this, Cassie.*

She removed her helm, her body reappearing the moment it was off her head, and set it on the floor. The metal made a tiny scrape against the concrete, and she winced at the sound. Her heart slammed in her chest as she listened for an alert or alarm from the army down the hall.

There was nothing.
~~~

Daphne exhaled. *Okay.* Her hands tightened around sword and shield. *You can do this. You can do this.*

Like an ancient Valkyrie, Daphne rounded the corner, brandishing the Harpe and screaming a war cry. The Crusaders gaped for a split second, then brought their entire arsenal to bear on her.

What the hell am I doing?! In slow-motion, Daphne watched as fingers tightened against triggers before she ducked her head and hid behind the great shield of Zeus.

Please be bulletproof! She knelt down so none of her body was visible behind the Aegis. *It's not like there were guns back then, so –"*

Her brow wrinkled. No bullets were striking the shield. No guns were firing. The hallway was quiet.

She peeked her head out from behind the shield, ready to pull it back at any sign of trouble.

What she saw left her speechless.

Each and every soldier had turned to stone. As Daphne stood and walked toward the barricades, she could see clear expressions of anger, confusion, and horror carved into marble, ebony, alabaster. Even their clothes and weapons had changed, seamless and perfect in every way, as if sculpted by a master.

"But...I don't..." Daphne shook her head. "What happened?"

"It was the Aegis, Daphne."

The familiar, yet terrifying, sound of Chloe's voice made Daphne jump and raise the shield once more. Her former roommate stood at the entrance to the hallway, in the door that Daphne had sought to pass.

"It won't work on me, though." Chloe pointed her blade at the Aegis, drawing Daphne's eyes to the shield. Engraved in the metal was a monstrous woman, her face contorted in rage and serpents attached to her scalp instead of hair.

"...Medusa?"

Chloe nodded, a crooked smile creeping over her lips. "It lost some of its power, being placed in Zeus' shield, you see." She turned and began walking into the room behind her. Daphne followed.

"What do you mean?"

"As you noticed, it didn't turn you to stone. Or me. Or any of the Gods of Olympus, for that matter. It simply doesn't have the strength to turn anyone possessed of real power."

The room they had entered was immense, with an arched ceiling and no windows. Large glass tubes filled with murky liquid lined the walls. Cords and wires were attached to each, feeding into a central receptacle—a black box in the middle of the floor.

Daphne looked around the room, then glanced at the small figure in her shirt pocket. Its beak pointed toward one of the tubes on the far wall.

She hitched her weapon and shield back up.

"Of course, when we met, I didn't know that you had power of any sort." Chloe shook her head. "You just seemed so...so *mundane*."

"Sorry to disappoint you." Daphne tried to swallow her fear. "So what now?"

Chloe laughed. "You think this is like one of your books, or a movie, maybe? You think I'm just going to give a huge villain's monologue and tell you about my master plan while you think of a way to defeat me?"

"Nope." Daphne pivoted, her sword arm coming over her shoulder and releasing the Harpe. The blade flew through the air, spinning end over end until it smashed into one of the tubes, breaking the glass and sending the dark liquid pouring over the ground.

Against the back of the container was Apollo. He was bound by dark filaments that resembled roots or veins and burrowed into and under his skin. His customary glow flickered, weak and wan, and he had lost most of his color.

Chloe's eyebrow rose, and she brought her hands together in mock applause. "Wonderful. You found him." Then her smile vanished, and her eyes lit up with crimson red. Daphne's breath caught in her chest when she saw what her adversary held in her hand—the radiant sphere that was Zeus' lightning. "So now he gets to watch you die."

A soft whisper, breath in Daphne's ear: "Get the Apple."

"Why?" Daphne drew back, covering her surprise by glancing at Apollo's limp form. She angled her body away from Chloe, hiding behind the Aegis and began rummaging in her pocket. "Why would you do this? What do you get out of it?"

Chloe lowered the sphere to her side, her eyes crinkling, tears appearing. "They *rejected* me, Daphne!"

The walls of the complex began to shake and small fissures appeared in the ground underneath her feet.

Daphne's fingers closed around the fruit in her pocket.

"They were supposed to be my family, but did they want me around? No. Did they ever consider that, maybe I was crying for help? That I was the victim of their elitism, of their pursuit of perfection?" She stretched her free hand toward Daphne. "Don't you understand?"

Daphne's hand ceased its movement, and she looked into Chloe's eyes. Instead of a vengeful god, she could still see the girl who liked Pepsi and hot guys in superhero movies.

But that girl had never existed.

"Bullshit." She pulled the Apple of Immortality from her pocket, hiding the action with an ostentatious wave of her other hand, moving the Aegis to block line of sight.

The tears and pleading disappeared from Chloe's face, like someone flicking a switch. "Fair enough." She laughed, all the cruelty and haughtiness returning as she raised the thunderbolt. "Then I guess it's just because I'm a bitch."

"Go!" The word was clear, sharp, and came from behind Chloe, but Daphne could not see who said it. Chloe spun around, searching for the source, and Daphne seized her chance. She turned, running across the expanse toward the tube where Apollo hung.

A laundry bag materialized over the angry goddess's head, covering her eyes. With a snarl, Chloe brandished the thunderbolt, and a pulse of electricity radiated out from her position in all directions, sparking off of the floor and ceiling in arcs of lightning. Daphne brought the Aegis up to shelter herself from the attack, but she heard a woman's scream and the sound of someone slamming into the wall.

Then she was shoving the Apple into Apollo's face. She had broken the skin with her nails, and the rich, translucent juice ran down his chin.

"Eat it, dammit! Hurry up!"

Chloe pulled off the charred remnants of the laundry bag, red eyes widening as she saw what was happening. As the first drips flowed into his mouth, his eyes snapped open and came alight. Sunfire roiled within them, and he took a large bite from the Apple.

Chloe ran toward the pair at impossible speed, her feet crashing into the ground, her strides covering three yards at a time.

It wasn't fast enough.

~~~

With the force of a nuclear explosion, sunfire rushed out of the tube Apollo had been held in. He strode forward, clad in his golden armor, and stretched out his hand. His bow materialized within his grasp, and he nocked a coruscating arrow to the string.

"You have failed, Eris." Apollo's power shone out across the room, stretching the shadows long in its wake. "I now know who was responsible, and you shall be punished for it."

"Punish me if you will, brother." Chloe pointed toward the chamber Apollo had just vacated. "But be sure to save some of your wrath for yourself."

"What do you—" Apollo glanced in the direction she indicated.

Daphne was stretched out at the foot of the tube, blown off her feet by the detonation. Her skin was charred black, her hair mostly gone. The hand which held the Aegis had been spared, but the contrast between her healthy skin and the ruin the rest of her body had become only served to make the sight more grisly.
~~~

The god's fury died in an instant. His eyes widened, moving from the nightmare at his feet back to Chloe, her mouth curled in a smirk.

"You—"

"No." The smirk widened. "*You.*"

It was a blow to the stomach; the sun god doubled over, his bow clattering to the floor, one end coming to rest on the snarling face of Medusa set in the Aegis. His mouth quivered, fought to form words, produced sobs instead.

"I...I didn't mean to hurt her." He fell to one knee. The smell of burning flesh touched his senses, triggering a wave of nausea. "I—"

Chloe stepped up, looking down at her fallen brother. "Of course you didn't." She pointed down at Daphne's corpse. "But you did it anyway, didn't you? Just like Troy."

"That was your fault!" Golden light blazed in Apollo's eyes. "And this! You bring ruin wherever you go, destroy everything you touch!"

Chloe came down to Apollo's level. For the first time, her smile seemed sad rather than mocking, and she laid a hand on Daphne's shield. "That's who I am. I make no apologies for it." Her gaze cut into Apollo's soul. "But you? God of healing, creativity, music? The glorious Apollo, epitome of manhood? You can't even protect the woman you love from yourself."

She laughed and stood. Apollo's eyes lingered over where Daphne's face had been, her lips now gone, her eyes boiled in her skull.

"Never to laugh again." He had lost all his strength, "Never to smile, or cry." He reached out, his fingers stopping a quarter of an inch from the remnants of her skin.

I never saw your book, my love. Tears welled in his eyes, choked his throat. *I wish I could have watched your face as you described each character, each scene. Why did I waste the time we had on sandwiches and prayers?*

"Begone." He turned his wet eyes on his sister. "Leave me to my grief, if you have even the smallest decency left to you.

"Or what?"

"Or I will kill you, here, now." He stood, his bow rising into his grasp. "I will destroy you, this building, and myself, dedicating the blaze as a funeral pyre."

Chloe's red eyes searched Apollo's golden ones, looking for a bluff.

She didn't find one.

"Enjoy your immortality, Shining One." Chloe spat on his face. "I think that, even without triumphing over you, I have won the war at last."

And she was gone, air rushing to fill the gap she left. Apollo breathed out, then laid his bow on the ground, wrapping his arms around Daphne's body and bringing her to his chest.

"I'm sorry." He kissed the charcoal of her forehead. "I'm sorry."

Chapter Twenty-Three

What is that smell?

Daphne opened her eyes. The sun was warm, shining clear in the sky, but the air was cool on her skin. The green grass tickled her feet as she sat up and brushed off the blades that had stuck to her blue dress.

She took a deep breath in through her nose. The rich, thick aroma of beef stew, complete with carrots, potatoes, and celery, flooded her senses, and she felt her mouth begin to water.

"Daphne!" Her mother's voice carried through the crisp afternoon air like a clarion call. "It's time for lunch!"

"Coming!" The young woman knelt down to scoop up her notebook and pen. She hurried down the hill, waving goodbye to her writing tree, a gorgeous willow whose branches drooped so low she had to push through them to leave.

"I'll see you later." Turning, she could see the smoke pouring from the fireplace of her home, a modest stone cottage by a river. A waterwheel turned in the gentle current, its creaking a comforting, familiar sound.

Daphne pulled the screen door open, reaching out to pet the small calico cat resting on a nearby shelf.

"Mom, that smells *so* good!" She dropped her notebook down on a countertop.

"Put that in the bookshelf, Daphne. You don't want to get stew on it."

Daphne rolled her eyes, but did as she was asked.

"So how's your book going, sweetie?" Her mother scooped some stew into a pair of pale blue bowls. Steam wafted over the soup, and Daphne could feel the warmth radiating from the bowl as she cupped her hands around it.

"Awesome! I got another two thousand or so written today. This place..." She looked out the window and sighed. "I don't know, Mom. It's just filling me with all these ideas!"

"Well, that's why your father and I waited to make sure you had a little getaway, somewhere you could escape to and be happy." Carolyn sat down across the table from her daughter, reached out, and took her hand. "When we found this place, well...we just knew."

"Yeah." Daphne spoke around a mouthful of stew. "Especially that willow tree up on the hill. I mean, that's like something out of a postcard."

Carolyn wrinkled her brow. "What willow tree?"

Daphne swallowed her chunk of potato. "You know." She gestured in the direction of her writing spot. "The one I go sit under while I work on my book."

Her mother shook her head and gave a gentle laugh. "I think you might need to take another look in that botany book you bought, sweetie. That's a laurel, not a willow!"

Daphne cocked an eyebrow. "Um, Mom? I know the difference between a willow and a laurel." She held up her hands above her head, then brought them down in great arcs to her sides.

"Willows have branches that go way up high, then rain down all over, like magic." Then she brought her hands in front of her and made a shaky outline of herself. "Laurels are like shrubs, almost. Not too tall, with bladed leaves. It's an evergreen."

Carolyn stared at her daughter for several seconds. "Are you picking on me or something?" She turned and pointed out the kitchen window. "Look at it!"

Daphne did. First she glanced, but when the glance did not return the expected information, she stood and walked to the window, staring at the tree the whole time.

It was a laurel, about ten feet tall, with one branch broken off on the side oozing sap.

"That...that's not possible." Her thoughts raced, keeping pace with her now adrenaline-fueled heart. "I...I was watching the sun through the branches. I had to brush past them on my way out." She looked again. "It was a goddamn willow tree!"

"Honey, calm down." Carolyn took her daughter by the shoulders and tried to lead her away from the window. "Maybe you just –"

Daphne forced her way out of her mother's grasp, running for the door. Thoughts bounced off the sides of her skull, careening in all directions. She ran all the way to the tree, stopping a few feet from it.

It can't be.

Her fingers ran over the leaves and bark. Tiny nicks and cuts appeared on her hands, but she did not feel any pain.

"The branches were right down here." Daphne ducked and dug her hands into the grass, pulling the blades out by the roots. "There was shade all over!" From her kneeling position, she looked up at the sun, now starting its trip down the dome of the sky. "Where did it go?"

She stood once more and paced around the tree, glaring at it, willing it to be what it should be.

Then something caught her eye. The broken branch.

My God. She reached up and touched the liquid that was congealing on the edge of the break. *That's not sap.* Her fingertips were stained red, and smelled of iron and copper. *It's blood.*

"Of course it is."

Like a hunted gazelle, Daphne's head swiveled as she searched for the intruding voice. It sounded familiar, but it came from...

She leaned in to the tree again.

"Is someone...is someone in there?" She touched the tree with her fingertips. "Hello?"

"Hello, Daphne. Nice to see you doing so well." The grain of the wood seemed to swirl in front of the young woman's eyes until it formed into a face—a face she knew well.

Her own.

Daphne fell to the ground, shock and fear gripping her heart. *I'm going crazy. I'm crazy. The tree is talking to me.*

The wooden lips moved. "You're not crazy. You're dead."

"Dead?" Daphne shook her head. "That...that doesn't make sense. I'm fine." She poked at herself, pinched a bit of skin on her arm. "And why am I talking to you?" She stood up and began to back away from the laurel. "You're a tree!"

"No." Wooden spikes, like extended roots, grew up from behind Daphne, poking her in the back as she tried to escape, hemming her in. "You must remember. We were one, you and I, until our death." The leaves moved, rustling in a non-existent wind. "But I was immortal, not so easily slain, so your mind pulled away from mine, to protect itself from the pain of eternity, of suffering."

Despite the insanity of the situation, the tree-thing's voice was soothing, calming. Daphne found herself beginning to relax. "Then why am I still here?"

Instead of answering, the creature countered with a question. "What do you remember about last week?"

"Umm..." Daphne thought, her brow creasing. "Relaxing. Writing. Having a good time at the river, swimming in the cold water. Why?"

"What about the week before?"

"About the same."

"Can you tell me exactly when it was you came to this place?"

Daphne nodded. "Of course I can. It was..."

Her voice trailed off. Her eyes widened, began to skitter across the landscape. *I can't remember. It's like...*

"It's like you've always been here, isn't it?" The tree-face was sympathetic. "With your mother always making you your favorite foods, working on that book that you love so much. If you were pressed, wouldn't you say that this was like your picture –"

"—Of Heaven." Daphne whispered the end of the creature's sentence, and it nodded, wood grain bending like muscle and hair. She could remember everything now—Eris, the Apple, the explosion. "Am I...am I in Heaven?"

The tree smiled. "Almost, my dear. These are the Elysian Fields, where the noble dead go when their threads are cut." The smile disappeared, replaced by a frown of fury. "But I should not be dead."

"What do you mean?" Daphne rubbed her arms; the cold was getting stronger. She looked up; the sky had clouded over and a wind had picked up, whipping her hair around her face.

"I am a spirit of the wood. A dryad. My life was an immortal one until my father 'saved' me by locking me within a tree. Because of him. Because of Apollo!" Thunder crashed and rain began to pelt down on the field.

"Daphne!" Carolyn's voice carried through the rain. "You should come in now! It's raining!"

"And again!" A branch moved toward Daphne, its twigs like fingers, reaching for her, grasping for her neck. "You follow him into the lair of Eris, like a sheep following its master. For what? Even if he were free, what does that mean? How does that change anything?" The wood of the branch began to scrabble at Daphne's clothes; she swatted the twigs to try to keep them off her. "Why was that worth my life?"

The wind was so strong now that Daphne was struggling to keep her feet. Her hair turned in this direction, then that, blinding her. The branches took hold of her, pinning her hands despite her struggles. The voice of the tree cut through the wind and booming thunderclaps, drilling into Daphne's ears, her mind.

"You have forfeited your right to this life!" The condemnation pressed on Daphne's shoulders, and she ceased her struggling, unable to free herself. "If not for you, I would have been immortal! If not for you and your infatuation, your lust, for Apollo, I would still live! If not-"

"Shut your mouth!" Daphne screamed into the swirling wind. "What would you have done with that life if you had had it? Stayed hiding from Eris forever? Cowered in fear?" She felt the grip of the branches and the intensity of the storm weaken, and she wrested her arms free, standing on her own two feet once again. "Maybe it was my decision that got us killed, but it was *my* life to give, damn it!"

"But not yours alone!" The reflection in the tree had grown dark with the rain, and its eyes were narrowed as it moved within the wood, darker, almost red within the brown. "You chose to risk our immortality for –"

"For him!" Daphne advanced on the tree and shoved a finger into the strange face. "And I would do it again! I would do it a thousand times over, because the world needs him. And..." The rain trailed off, a monsoon to a drizzle, and Daphne's voice went with it. "...And because I need him."

A pause as the clouds cleared and the sun reemerged. The face in the tree was incredulous. "You...you would truly give up eternal life, never having to face death, to ensure that he lived?" Daphne nodded, tears welling in her eyes. "Even if you never got to see him again?"

The young woman held her head up high. "I would."

"Why?"

She smiled, a genuine expression of warmth and happiness. "Because he deserves it. Because he makes the world a better place by being in it." She wiped the moisture from her face. "Because I'm happy knowing that I died saving his life."

"No no no!" A ring of clouds closed in, surrounding the sunlit tree like a tightening noose. "He takes what he wants and casts it away!" The tree-face snapped its teeth as it screamed. "You think that he cares for you? The arrow in his heart makes him love you, makes him watch you walk, makes him stare at your face. His affections are false, artificial, un-true…and you sacrificed yourself for that! For a lie!"

Daphne shook her head. "I didn't save him so he would love me. I did it because I couldn't do anything else."

Her reflection in the wood began to cackle. "He tore apart those who dared claim they were more skilled than he, and cursed others for disagreeing with him! How does a man like that make the world a better place? How is a man like that worth saving?" A thunderclap. "Can an immortal being, all-powerful, truly change who he is?"

Daphne felt her throat close in tandem with the swirling ring of storm clouds. *What if she's right? What if it was all an act?* She looked back up at the tree. *What if he hasn't changed at all?*

The sunlight began to falter again as wisps of grey sought to cover it forever more. "There is one thing, Daphne." The tree's branches spread, like arms. "An immortal is difficult to kill, and the Fates have not yet claimed our thread. I will leave you here, and go on to live my life, forever." The figure in the wood stretched upward, changing from a face to a full-figured dryad, who looked down and smiled a cruel, heartless smile.

"And when I get there, Apollo will love me, and I will rebuff him, crushing his heart."

Daphne watched, her chest hitching, as the dryad raised its arms toward the top of the tree, and the leaves stretched themselves toward the sky. Above the tree formed a rift, a tear, almost like a zipper opening, and on the other side was darkness.

And sobbing.

Daphne felt something stir in her chest. She held a hand to her heart, the beat steady under her palm. She glanced back to the dryad.

And saw the leaden arrow.

All at once, realization crashed in on her, galvanizing her muscles and bones. She hurled herself at the tree, climbing it as fast as she could, racing the dryad moving through the wood to the top.

"What are you doing?" The tree spirit sounded panicked, worried. "Get down!"

"No way in hell, you crazy bitch." Daphne spat out a mouthful of leaves and kept climbing. "The way I see it, there's only room for one of us, and it's sure not going to be you!"

The dryad shrieked in rage, flowing upward. The tree branches kept growing, kept rising to the rift in the heavens. She was almost there.

She's going to get there first. Daphne's foot slipped, but she held on despite the slivers digging into her hands. *Unless...*

"You're wrong, you know." Daphne stopped moving and wiped her brow, propping herself in the fork of a branch. "He won't love you. He'll know the difference."

The dryad stopped, the branches thickening around the portal. "How? He is besotten by the golden arrows. He can do nothing else."

"Well, sure. He might love *me* because of the arrow." Daphne reached up and put her hand on a branch the thickness of her wrist. *God, I hope this works.* "But not you. You're not as pretty as I am."

The wood seemed to smoulder in the dryad's eyes. "What did you say? I am eternal, a spirit of the forest and wood itself! No mere mortal could compare! Only the gods –"

"And yet, he wants me, a mortal woman." She swung her other hand up to the branch; now she was standing with her feet planted on two different areas, wedged into forks. "A god wants me. If it wasn't for the arrow, he never would have been interested in you, anyway." Daphne laughed. "I guess you didn't measure up."

The dryad hissed, sweeping back down toward her. The branch she held began to grow spikes, causing her to bite her lip to stifle the scream. Blood trickled down from her palms.

"What do you know?" Its face stopped in front of hers, its eyes filled with rage, with hatred. "How dare you –"

Daphne gave voice to the pain and the sudden effort she was making, the sound overwhelming whatever the dryad was going to say, as her muscles tensed. The blood poured, and the *crack* of breaking wood resounded like a gunshot.

Red sap coursed out of the broken branch like a river. Daphne threw the wood to the ground and spat in the dryad's face as it contorted in pain. She shrieked three, four, five times...then vanished, as if she had never been there.

Daphne reached up and resumed the climb.

The pain was intense, and she could see the world pulsing around her field of vision, beginning to bleach out. Black and white crept into the world of color, but she forced herself upward until the portal, the tear, was within reach.

Her hand, covered in her own crimson blood, reached up through the gap in space and time. It touched a hard concrete floor, but began to slide backward as Daphne's muscles gave way.

The world went black.

No! It swam back into focus, and her fingers gripped the nearest branch to keep from falling off. She looked back up at the gate, and the pain vanished, and a smile, so wide it threatened to escape her face, took the place of her grimace.

The golden god was leaning in through the gate, holding out his hand for hers, his soul visible and longing for her, afraid for her.

Loving her.

His warm fingers closed against hers and, with one smooth motion, he pulled her up and into his arms. She looked into his face, and he into hers. He kissed her forehead, and she felt a hot pulse leap through her body, centering on her wounds. The open punctures vanished, and Daphne felt her strength return.

"Daphne, I-"

"Later." She wrapped her arms around him, pressing her mouth against his. All the bottled-up longing of the past several days, coupled with the fear and worry of the last twenty-four hours, surged to the fore. He tasted like jasmine tea and honey, and Daphne couldn't get enough, pulling at him with all her strength, trying to pull herself into him as their lips moved against each other's. After what could have been a minute and could have been an hour, she pulled away, panting, her eyes searching his face, her mind reeling from the cataclysmic collision of emotions.

"I love you."

Apollo seemed equally stunned. "I...Are..."

"She's fine." Cassandra's voice came from behind Apollo, and Daphne shifted to see her friend sitting on the floor, back against the wall. She was grinning, although her eyes were still covered by bandages. "Can't you tell?"

"Cassie!" Daphne broke free from Apollo and ran to the Seeress, almost knocking her over as she knelt and grabbed her in a bear hug. "I'm so glad you're okay!" She pulled back, confusion on her face.

"But how? I heard you hit the wall after she blasted you with lightning."

"Thanks to him." Cassandra nodded at Apollo. "You'd be amazed what the god of medicine can do in a place fully stocked with supplies and equipment."

Daphne hugged her again as Apollo approached them. "Well, you were great! I couldn't believe it when I saw that bag appear on her head!"

She turned to Apollo. "And I think you know how I feel, Sun God. How about you?" He blinked, so she poked him in the chest, but she was smiling, teasing. "Does what you said on Olympus still stand?"

Apollo took a deep breath, gathering his wits, then nodded. "Of course it does, but...aren't you worried that –"

"That you only love me because of the arrow?" He nodded. "No. Because I learned something very important while I was..." She shuddered. "While I was dead."

Apollo took her hands and kissed them, his warmth banishing the chill from her body. "What did you learn, love?"

"That I am not Daphne." There was a pause. "At least, not the Daphne that you saw when Eros shot you."

Apollo shook his head. "You are. You resemble her exactly. You have her memories, now, do you not? How can you say you are not she?"

Daphne laughed and helped Cassandra to her feet. "It's simple, really. Eros asked the Fates to bring her back because he felt bad about what he had done, but the Fates can't create life. They can only end it, or alter its destiny, so they had to splice her thread onto a new one. Mine." She tapped her chest. "My heart was never pierced by his arrow, Apollo, so I never hated you. When I realized that, I also realized –"

Cassandra smiled. "You realized that he had never been shot looking at you."

Apollo's eyes were wide. "You mean...you mean that his power...is ended?"

"Yes." Daphne looked up at him again. "And that's why I would like to be with you now, Apollo. I love you, and if you love me, it's not because of magic."

"And I do." Apollo kissed her again, with less ardor but the same affection.

"What happened to Eris?" Daphne looked around. "Did she run away?"

Apollo's eyes darkened, and he stepped back. "Daphne, there is something you need to see."

Daphne's brow furrowed. "What is it?"

Apollo moved into the middle of the room and pressed a button on the central receptacle. Lights began flickering to life inside each of the tubes. Daphne stared in a mixture of wonder and horror as the contents of each were revealed.

Bodies. The bodies of gods.

I recognize them—Zeus, Ares. Athena. The gods were floating in the same liquid that had held Apollo, with the same tendrils locked into their flesh, but they were in far worse condition. Large pieces of them were missing—Zeus' arm, Hephaestus' legs— and they were, all of them, withered and desiccated, as if the very fluid was being drained from them by the vein-like growths within them.

Daphne moved in a circle, her eyes wide and jaw agape. *It's not only the Gods...everyone they took, everything they caught.* Satyrs and nymphs and all manner of other spirits, all held in the same terrible stasis. The tendrils pulsated, feeding off of them, and Daphne suppressed a gag.

"Are they...are they still alive?"

Apollo nodded, his face grim. "They are, although they may not be aware of it." He sighed. "At least, I hope they are not."

"Yeah." Daphne looked back toward Apollo, and what she saw—despair, hopelessness—burned in her heart. "Isn't there anything you can do?"

Apollo shook his head. "When I..." He tried to smile at Daphne, but it was tremulous and weak. "When you saved me, the same fire that –"

"That killed her!" Cassandra's voice came from the back like a hail-Mary pass.

Apollo winced. "It also burnt up the Apple of Immortality. If that had survived, then maybe they could be saved, but I know of no other way."

Daphne's face fell. "I'm sorry. I didn't know—"

"You have nothing to apologize for." He turned off the lights, once more shrouding his kin in darkness. "If it were not for you, none of us would live."

She took a breath. "That's not good enough." She strode to Apollo's shattered prison. Everything was covered by the suspension fluid, so she went by feel, running her fingers on each object.

Please let it be here. Please...Yes!

Her hand came up with a tiny, crisped husk of fruit, scorched black on the outside. Her heart sank. *It's totally destroyed.* She poked at it, looking for a spot that might have been shielded from the blast. *There's no fruit left at all.*

Something rattled within. Daphne shook the remains of the Apple. The same sound.

"I think...I think these are seeds!" With trembling fingers, Daphne peeled apart the blackened layers until she had opened up the core. "Yes!" She cupped them in the palm of her hand--three tiny, glistening seeds. Unburnt. Undamaged.

And tiny shoots began to curl out of them as Daphne held them in her grasp.

Daphne and Apollo exchanged glances, then the woman laid one of the seeds on the ground. She focused on it, channeling the energy of the green things, of the wild plants of the world.

Grow. She held her hand over it, feeling the struggles within the seed coat, hearing the fibers stretching. *Come on. Grow!*

Roots dug into the ground, spreading in a circle. Daphne began to sweat under the effort, droplets pattering on the floor, her perspiration feeding the new tree as the seedling began to rise up.

Triumph filled her soul. *Yes! Grow!* She wiped her brow, poured her energy into the plant.

The roots and leaves began to retreat.

Her eyes widened, and she redoubled her effort, but the tree kept shrinking, a time-lapse video played in reverse until all that was left was a seed again.

Daphne collapsed onto the ground, hitting it with her hand, ignoring the pain shooting up her arm.

Apollo knelt down beside her, embracing her as she sobbed. "It's all right, love. It's all right. You tried."

"Why isn't it working?" Daphne cried into his chest. "It was working! What's wrong?"

"It's the Tree of Immortality, Daphne." Apollo stroked her hair; his own eyes were red and sad, but his voice was calm and soothing. "Perhaps a dryad's power simply isn't enough."

Cassandra stepped up close to them, her hands in front of her body. She touched Apollo's head and came down beside the couple. "Earth and Sun bring forth the fruit of the Gods."

Apollo's head snapped to the side and he stared at Cassandra as he completed the verse. "And in golden celebration do they feast."

Daphne pulled back a little, looking from the one to the other of them. "What...what do you mean?"

Apollo stood, helping Daphne to her feet. "Cassandra has remembered what must be done, my love."

Cassandra kissed Daphne on the forehead. "This is the will of the Moirae, that you restore the balance. Do this now."

Apollo held her hands in his, fingers interlaced. "Help it grow."

Daphne inhaled Apollo's scent, shivering as the sensations raced down her back, then bowed her head and reached out once more to the seeds. She could feel them begin to stretch out once again, but, as before, they reached a certain point and then began to retreat.

She cried out in frustration, and Apollo nodded. "Now it's my turn."

The God of the Sun began to glow, soft, warm waves of golden light like ripples on a pond, spreading from his body, banishing the cold from the room and filling it with his healing power. All the creative energy that flowed from the Sun was Apollo's to command, and he did so now, in gentle pulses.

Daphne reveled in the power, in the warmth. She molded herself to his body, and allowed her own energy to meld with his in the same way. Her eyes were closed, and her only sensation was the totality of her connection with him...and his with her.

I love you, Apollo. The thought came without warning.

And I love you, Daphne.

She opened her eyes wide, and met his, finding them just as astonished but pleased. The green swam in the blue, and the blue lost itself in the green.

"A-hem." Cassandra's voice interrupted their reverie. "I think you can turn it off, now. It's big enough."

Daphne turned. "What do you –"

The seed had sprouted and grown into a massive specimen, easily twenty feet tall, with many heavy golden fruits hanging from its branches.

She smiled up at Apollo. "Come on. We've got work to do."

Epilogue

Daphne hurried through the streets of Olympus, waving to the spirits and functionaries she had helped to save three months ago. *God, I still feel so out of place sometimes.* She looked down at her royal-blue evening dress, then back at the variety of togas and strange apparel that the residents wore.

She arrived at the entrance to the great hall where Apollo had brought her for food and stories on her first visit to the great city. The door was closed, but Daphne could feel the power and presence behind it. *I hope I'm not too late.*

She brought her hand up to knock, and the door opened as her knuckles made contact with it. The outrush of air brought with it the rich aromas of meats and fruits, almost lifting her away in ecstasy just from the smell. She fought back the sudden onset of salivation and stepped into the hall.

Arrayed around the giant table were seated the Dodekatheon—at the head of the table was mighty Zeus, the air about him stirring like the onset of a storm. To his right was lovely Hera, his sister and wife, and she smiled when she saw Daphne enter the room. Across from Hera was grey-eyed Athena, a snowy owl on her chair and her armor and weapons close at hand. She nodded when Daphne caught her eye.

The rest were there as well—Poseidon, skin caked with sea salt, and Ares, hard and grim yet full of power and life. Hephaestus was attended by two Cyclopes who were carrying him, with his withered legs dangling from their arms but a happy grin on his face. Aphrodite was beside him, gorgeous, voluptuous, sensuality flowing off of her with her every gesture. Her eyes moved from Ares to gaze at Daphne, triggering a twinge of sexual heat within her.

A wild, beautiful woman with a silvery bow propped up on the table was talking to a younger man with a serpent-entwined staff and winged sandals on his feet, with quick words and a bright, easy smile. When Daphne looked closer at the woman, she recognized something in the shape of her face, the evenness of her teeth, the mannerisms of her speech, and laughed. *I guess even godly siblings are alike, aren't they?*

A more sedate presence, Demeter waited with her hands folded in her lap, nodding to acknowledge Daphne's entrance into the room and beckoning her to come forward. Beside her, Dionysus held up an ever-full cup of red wine, toasting her without words, then tipping it back to drain, the crimson fluid pouring down his neck and bare chest as well as his throat.

Daphne stood in the doorway for several seconds. *They're...they're all so beautiful.* Adrenaline pushed its way into her veins, and she could feel herself begin to sweat. *They must think I look ridiculous.*

"I think you look lovely."

Daphne turned her head to see Apollo entering the hall behind her. He wore what Daphne had come to call his "evening wear," a gold and white tunic, embroidered so that it shone in the light, emblazoned with his symbol on the chest. It was loose-fitting, but left no doubt as to the shape of the man underneath, and Daphne could feel the desire awakened by Aphrodite sharpen and take focus.

Apollo stepped up and slipped his arm through hers. The assembled Olympians quieted as the two approached the empty seats at the table. The silence was a powerful contrast to the gaiety and levity of moments ago.

Then Zeus, King of the Gods, stood and began to applaud.

Each member of the Dodekatheon followed suit, and although every one applauded differently—Hephaestus was enthusiastic, Hera dignified, Dionysus a little sloppy and overcheerful—the act brought Daphne to the edge of tears, her throat choking. Apollo tightened his grip for a moment, then stepped away from her. When she glanced over, he brought his hands together and joined his family.

For over a minute, the Gods clapped, as did all the functionary spirits and attendants in the hall, giving voice to their appreciation. When they stopped, the applause trickling away, Zeus spread his hands wide, and his voice boomed out over the group.

"I now call this, the first Council of Olympus, into session." He motioned for Daphne and Apollo to sit. "This is the first time we have been here since Eris' betrayal, and the world has changed. There is much to discuss."

"Like oil spills and shark hunting." Poseidon tightened his grip on his trident and salt fell from his hand onto the table. Athena nudged him with an elbow.

"Yes." Zeus opened his hand toward Daphne and Apollo. "But for our first order of business, the Council wishes to honor the courage and strength of Daphne Gianakos."

Hades stood. "Without you, we would still be consigned to an endless death."

Demeter was next. "Without you, the Earth itself would suffer and die."

Hephaestus drew himself up in his dais. "Because of you, we have another chance to live, to breathe, to create."

Dionysius swayed as he stood. "Without you, I'd never hold a party like this again!"

Hera scowled at him before turning back to the guest of honor. "Because of you, my family lives again. I will be eternally grateful."

Poseidon raised his trident. "Because of you, the orca and dolphin will soon be free, and the seas cleansed, and –"

Hermes broke in, chuckling at his uncle. "Ahem. Thanks to you, the world will once more know us, and we will watch over it forever."

Ares' armor clanged as he moved. "And I'll get to learn about all these new toys." He cracked his knuckles. "Do you know where I can get hold of one of those thermonuclear bombs?"

"Brother." Athena shook her head, then raised her glass. "Daphne, because of you, disaster is averted. You have fulfilled your destiny and restored the balance, and all owe their lives to you."

Apollo brushed a loose strand of Daphne's hair back behind her ear. "And without you, my life would still be hollow and empty." He waved his hand out toward the table. "You gave me back my family, and you took away my heart."

Tears were flowing down Daphne's cheeks. She tried to speak, but her throat remained closed and the words emerged in stutters obscured by sobs. Ares rolled his eyes, then flinched as if he had been struck.

"I...I..."

Zeus' voice boomed out once again. "And that is why we have, all of us, decided to bestow upon you the greatest gift that is in our power to grant." He waved his hand and a new chair, formed of living, twining wood, materialized next to Apollo's. "A seat on our council, and an immortal life as Goddess of the Written Word, first among the Muses, with all the power and responsibility that comes with it."

Artemis rose from her seat and walked over to Daphne. Both her gait and her gaze were like a wild animal, a panther perhaps, as she looked the woman up and down. She stood for several heartbeats before speaking.

"My brother has chosen well." She drew a hand across Daphne's cheek, trailing a fingertip down to her blouse...then gripping it with a tight fist and drawing her close. "But if you hurt him, I will hunt you down and end you."

"Calm, sister." Apollo's hands moved in to separate Artemis from Daphne. "I can take care of myself, thank you." He turned to Daphne, smiled, then knelt before her.

No way.

"I cannot offer you immortality as a God, Daphne." Apollo reached into a pocket and brought forth a shining ring, gold encrusted with gems that looked like diamonds but which glowed from the inside. "But I can offer you my own life for all eternity. Will you join me, here, now and forever as my wife and partner?"

Daphne took three deep breaths, feeling the weight of the Olympians' gazes on her. When she felt she had calmed enough to speak through the knot in her throat, she leaned down and kissed Apollo.

"Yes. Yes, I will."

Apollo stood and embraced Daphne as the hall erupted into cheers. Dionysus began distributing wine to the attendees and the satyrs began piping a tune. Dancing broke out and each Olympian came to congratulate the two lovers. Hermes cut in on Apollo and swept Daphne off her feet for several minutes before returning her to the Sun God.

When there was a pause in the festivities, Daphne pulled Apollo away from the main party. She was smiling so much that her face hurt.

"What is it, Daphne?" His eyes were so warm and full of love. "Is something wrong?"

"No, nothing's wrong. It's just..." She licked her lips. "When they...when they make me a god, what will that involve?"

"Ah." Apollo waved his hand like someone presenting a hidden prize. "It is simple for us and painless for you. You will stand before the Council, and Zeus will invest you with immortality. True immortality, unlike before." He took her hand in his. "There is no need to fear."

"Oh, I'm not afraid. It's something else." She was bobbing up and down, excitement evident in every gesture.

"Then what?"

"I'm just not sure if they should make me immortal before or after our daughter is born." She looked up into his face, watching as recognition and realization struck and the amazed smile stretched his lips.

"Our...daughter?"

"I took a test this morning." She bowed her head, looking up at her man over the frames of her glasses. I hope you don't mind, but I told Cassie."

Apollo shook his head, still grinning. "What did she say?"

"She already knew, of course. Said it was going to be a girl—that's how I found that out." Daphne squeezed his hands. "What do you think?"

Apollo swept down and picked her up, his hands wrapped around her waist as he spun her in the air. "I think that the next Olympian is going to have the best mother in the world." He brought her down to his lips and kissed her again.

Daphne nuzzled his neck, taking small nips of his skin. "I wouldn't mind, you know, practicing for the next one. I've missed you these last couple of days."

Apollo laughed. "And I you. But I think we have an announcement to make and a party to return to."

Daphne thrust her lip in a fake pout, but it didn't last long. "Fine. But you're coming to my place afterward." She poked him in the chest. "No excuses!"

"I wouldn't dream of making excuses." Apollo took her arm and turned back toward the entrance to the hall. "Shall we?"

"Yes." Daphne leaned into his shoulder. "We shall. Forever."

END